The Marriage Seat

By the same author

TEN POEMS ANALYSED
CARNIVAL
SCHOOLBOY RISING

NIGEL FOXELL

The Marriage Seat

THE HARVESTER PRESS

A Harvester Novel
First published in 1978 by
THE HARVESTER PRESS LIMITED
Publisher: John Spiers
2 Stanford Terrace, Hassocks, Sussex

© Nigel Foxell, 1978

British Library Cataloguing in Publication Data

Foxell, Nigel
 The marriage seat.
 I. Title
 823'.9'1F   PR9199.3.F6M/

 ISBN 0–85527–771–8

Set and printed by Bristol Typesetting Co. Ltd.,
Barton Manor, St. Philips, Bristol

CHAPTER I

Supper for six, hot from the Baby Belling, plates hot too; *too* hot, scorching my guest's thighs. One of the women said it was quite *outchy*; and her husband, a director of Crunch and Child, made a joke about hot pants.

I shrugged. 'Have you ever given a party where something didn't go wrong?'

'Ah,' they assured me, 'that's the secret of success.'

Perhaps. Something must go wrong to take minds off things that go wrong. Doesn't a child ask his parents to hide so that he can lose the fear of losing them?'

'You haven't got such a thing as a *tray*, have you?'

'Only the ice-tray.'

Laughter. At least *that*. Embarrassed at seeing me after ages, what could they say? In desperation I'd switched on TV, a celebrity was being interviewed about his divorce, he suddenly broke down and wept, it was one of those chances that the media pray for, it made terribly good viewing.

And now came that knuckle-tap on the door of my bedsit. Only the ice-tray, I'd said. And they'd laughed. They would have laughed longer if it hadn't been for that knuckle-tap. Creak of boot on landing. Scratch of walky-talky. Then a knuckle-tap.

'Yes?'

'*Yes*' didn't mean '*Come in*', the door had a lock. My key, working on the landlady's master, was restricted, which meant I couldn't cut it for my friends, not that I had any, I had guests instead.

Who was it? Let him wait. Or go away. Either it's urgent or he'll go away.

But he *won't* go away, it *is* urgent, because he's a Bobby, see? I know it's a Bobby, I'd have known it without the walk, without the walky-talky. I ask who it is, *Who is it*? But who am I deceiving?

Those guests watch the way I put down my plate on the carpet. Why am I so casual about the putting of my plate on the carpet?

Another knock. *All* right.

In the dark of the half-landing he's a draught of cold air, his badge is ice against my face.

Wanted a word with me . . . sir.

'Let's have a bit of sunshine,' I said, pressing the time switch. 'Good evening. Did someone ring 999? I can't think what for. Except that the plates were damned hot. Sorry, it's an ambulance we need; or the fire brigade.'

I winked at my guests, but they didn't notice, they were looking at the floor, at the linoleum between the wall and the carpet.

Between the wall and the wall-to-wall carpet.

Linoleum. They hadn't noticed it till the Bobby came. Why had he come? Did he have to come *now*? I was giving a party, it was the first I'd given since . . .

O.K., I shouldn't have given a party with the linoleum showing, but (please) the room isn't mine, I've only rented it, the landlady's the one to punish, not the tenant. Tenant means victim, you don't punish the victim.

I was punished already. Because of the linoleum. They'd never have noticed it but for the Bobby. Half an inch of linoleum. Centimetre. Not even linoleum, but a cracked, frayed centimetre. Sounds like an insect. A dead insect.

Dead? Couldn't I see—my guests had seen—it was snaking under the carpet, cracking and fraying as far as their feet and my plate, a carpetful of centimetres to crawl up their evening out!

From my belly came one of those despairs I'd learnt to live with; would never learn to live with: despairs at—I hardly know what—at missed buses; mould on the bread; bottle-tops that won't unscrew.

And the scratch-scratch of that walky-talky.

Even the air of the landing had an imprisoned look, like the face of a child that's about to give way to sorrow.

Already, reader, if you've read this far, you're (I can hear you) snickering over the fuss that I, a grown man, make about trifles. (Odd) it's only the big things I've learnt to bear with any kind of calm. The Bobby should've said, straightaway: 'I've come to arrest you!' Then my blood wouldn't have raced with such panic from my heart.

'I have guests,' I said. 'What do you want?'

He unbuttoned his breast pocket and slowly produced a pad. You must be a Bobby to move as slowly as that.

'Can I have a word with you, sir? Privately.'

'Privately? In a bedsit?'

'On the landing then.'

The metal of his helmet. The cold of the common parts. Smell of aspidistra. Stale dust.

I said: 'Trouble, presumably, with one of the other tenants.'

He shook his head, he'd come to see me about my wife, that's what that head-shake said, he wanted me for murdering her; not that I had, or even tried, not yet, but I'd given it thought. Given it thought! Wished it passionately, planned it painstakingly. And the law knew this, would call contemplation 'murder', you've to take the Bible in your right hand.

7

'It's about your wife,' he said.

I would be taken into preventive detention.

'Wife?' I said, frowning, as if the word were one I hadn't heard for a very long time. 'But my wife doesn't live here. If you wish to see my wife, she's in North Kensington, at Chivalry House.'

I'd been there at noon, I'd gone to pick up the child, it was Saturday, I used to see him every weekend. But today she wouldn't let me, which was contrary to the agreement, she had put herself in the wrong. And she wouldn't have set a Bobby on me when it was she who'd been in the wrong. Maybe he wanted me to testify against her; except that he couldn't have known what she'd done, he must be wanting me for that murder I hadn't yet committed.

But part of my mind was telling me I *had* committed it, though that was later, when she was my wife no longer, which makes a difference; I mean you won't start thinking I'm the usual kind who's too scared to say he's leaving, it's simpler to kill.

The time-switch went out as he was writing, I pressed it again for the Bobby's sake, I've always hated light, I hate violence of any kind. Said : 'A woman like my wife, with no man about the place, it's as well if the police keep an eye on her, I'm grateful.'

He glanced at my suit as if it might provide evidence against me. At my tie, my slippers.

'Did you enter her house?'

So she'd . . .

Today, in the quiet of my cell, I can look back on this with a calmer hatred. And yet I'm no nearer to explaining how she could've brought that forefinger to dial those three nines. Apparently she thought that mercy, being a divine attribute, should not be usurped by mortals.

I smiled. I can't think why I smiled. I suppose it was the

8

smile at finally banging my head on the ceiling of the world.

Suddenly I felt suffocated, the air was hate and fumes, a plane roared overhead, and the roar entered me like a poison, I shook. The house shook, too.

'Men're murdering their wives,' I said, 'and babies're being battered; yet you find time to call on me, just because I . . .'

'Yes, sir.'

I ('No!' I said) *could not* believe it; she'd (all right, all right) behaved like that before, but . . .

Mothers don't behave like that.

The Bobby frowned into the deep blue of his serge, which thickened, stiffened, supporting him in his puzzlement. 'By saying "no", do you mean you weren't there?'

'Yes. I was.'

And she'd sent the law after me.

'Look,' I said, 'this is a party I'm giving, you've interrupted a party. So be brief, please. Or else let the matter ride till morning. O.K.?'

But he took his time; wrote down all the details of my visit to what was once the family house. And told me I was under arrest.

'Arrest?'

He nodded. I would be handed over to the sergeant for interrogation.

My poor child! All the way to the police station I kept saying *poor child.* My guests I forgot about, I could only think of that child.

He himself would already have been interrogated by this Bobby. Your father entered the house; and then what? And then? And then? But he'd answered well, brave boy. The Bobby told me how well he'd answered, I specially asked if he'd answered well.

'And he seemed all right?'

'Yes.'

A*   9

Yes, he was *my child* : only trifles ever crumpled him. But in a crisis he was stout. Stout at the time, that is. And after? What was he thinking *now*, in bed and awake? What would he think when his mother told him I'd been arrested? For she would tell him, surely, as soon as she heard. If not sooner.

'Your father's been arrested.'

Sweet woman. You've seen her in the paper, this beauty, blonde and petite. A mother too. Murdered.

But not yet. It took some doing. In many ways she treated the child so well. I don't know how I can best describe the dilemma I was in : it was as if—this may sound (is) far-fetched, but I can think of nothing closer—as if you were to contemplate all the filth and hardship of industrialism, decide that the world would be better if we did without the last hundred and fifty years; and then remembered modern medicine, or miracle wheat.

I'm at the police station, they look interested, they aren't used to seeing my sort.

I'm so glad they're interested. If I'd had a book in my pocket, a single *Georgic*, I might've tried to read. And there was not so much as a Notice on the walls, or a Wanted photograph. One single *graffito* : I love thy very shit.

By the way, I was honest when I said I forgot about my guests. I could safely entrust them to their expressions of sorrow, for you know the old saying as well as I do : Cry and the world cries with you; laugh and you laugh alone.

Let's hope my cat's all right.

I was brought before the sergeant.

'Sit down,' he said. 'Now tell me : did you at noon enter your wife's home?'

My answer was : 'I entered Chivalry House.'

'Is that where she lives?'

'Yes.'

'You entered her home, then.'

'Yes, I entered the family home.'

He paused to consider. 'The . . . family . . . But I thought you and your wife were estranged.'

'My child's there.'

'Your child's there because his mother has care and control.'

'Yes; but I see my child every weekend.'

'By mutual agreement?'

'By agreement between counsel.'

'I see. By mutual agreement. But let's be sensible about this : if the child's ill, you can't expect your wife to let him go out.'

'The child was *not* ill,' I said. And I could feel the hatred in my own eyes, the sergeant was seeing things from my wife's point of view. 'Would I have taken him out if he'd been ill?'

'Listen. I'm not concerned whether the child was ill or not—'

'*Well, I am.*'

At once he gave me a warning look. I wasn't to shout; wasn't to interrupt.

'Regardless,' he said, 'whether the child was *ill* or not, you can't go forcing your way into other people's homes.'

'Except that in my particular case . . .'

'What's so particular?'

'Sergeant,' I said, leaning across the desk to him. My tone was frank, man-to-man. He'd be flattered by this. What's more, unlike the Bobby who'd called on me he was no boy, so if luck was on my side he wouldn't keep to the book.

'Please, sergeant, listen to me for a minute. Have you (you don't mind my asking, I hope) any children of your own?'

'I have eight,' he replied with some vigour.

'Eight. Really. Now suppose, sergeant, one of *your* children was in somebody else's home. And he got ill. You

11

wanted to see how he was. Right? But the person in charge of him tried to keep you away. What would you do? Would you say to yourself, "I'm scared to set foot inside, I could be arrested and charged with unlawful entry." Or would you say: "I love that child. I'm going to see how he is." '

The sergeant frowned; remained silent for some time. 'You . . . (surely) said your child was *not* ill.'

'He wasn't. But I'd been told he *was*.'

'Who by?'

'By my wife. It was my wife who came to the door. She said: "You can't take him out, he's ill." "Ill?" I said. "Then I'd better see how he is." But she barred the way. I said: "The child's ill, so let me get by, I want to say hello to him." She replied: "He *isn't* ill." I said: "Not ill? That's funny, you've just told me he's ill." '

'And what did she say?'

'She said: "Get out!" '

'And did you?'

'No. If the child was ill I should be visiting him, seeing how he was; and if he was well he should be spending the weekend with me.'

'Poor child,' said the sergeant without any change of inflexion. 'Poor child.'

I loved him for that.

Next moment he was back to his questioning.

'And your son, where was *he*, all this time?'

'That's the whole point, he was nowhere to be seen. Why hadn't he run to greet me? I said to her: "Why hasn't he run to greet me?" She said: "Because he's afraid of you." I said: "If he's afraid of me, it's because you've *made* him afraid of me." '

The sergeant's head veered irritably to one side: 'Oh, come on!'

I looked at him with calm eyes, uttering a central truth of

12

my existence. 'That woman would do anything to hurt me.'

'And *she*,' he replied, carefully folding his hands in imitation of my own calm, 'claims *you* hurt *her*. She claims (so I'm told) that you threw her against the wall.'

'Sergeant, she came at me with a cigarette.'

'A cigarette?'

'All right, it sounds ridiculous, but the cigarette was alight, she tried to stub it in my face.'

'And you reacted by throwing her against the wall.'

'I did nothing of the sort.'

He leant back; flipped the clip of his ball-point pen, it was a most irritating habit of his.

'I'm astonished. I'm astonished because . . . she had a witness.'

'Who?'

'Her child.'

'My *child*, you say?'

He nodded. 'I'm afraid so. And as it's improbable that an eight year-old would lie . . .'

'O God!'

I was more praying than swearing. I felt sick; sick with sorrow at my child's bewilderment, the bewilderment! I could see it more clearly than if he'd been before me, more intensely than if dreaming. It was all I thought about, I didn't even think of telling the sergeant that my child was alone in one of the bathrooms on an upper floor, I eventually found him alone in one of the bathrooms on an upper floor. Standing there. Just standing by the bath. 'My child!' I said. I bent down and took him in my arms, I'd have liked to squeeze him into me, make him part of me, not leave him in separateness to face that woman. Gently I asked him why he was standing in the bathroom—of all places; and he said Mummy had put him there, told him not to move till she came back. 'Never mind!' I said, in the fatuous way that

13

parents do; and I picked him up in a passion of tenderness, such tenderness as I'd never known before. Or such fury. And the tenderness was itself a fury. Meantime my wife hadn't moved from the hall, she stood there waiting and alert. I said : 'Care to try and stop me?' My voice was so quiet and calm, almost caressing. But the look in my eyes told another story : there too was a caress, but it was the kind of caress, exquisite and long-drawn-out, with which I finally came to murder her.

So she let me pass. Not a word. Not even the thrust of a lighted cigarette.

And for a moment I felt a certain sweet self-satisfaction, though it was quite unjustified, for I should really have murdered her there and then. Why not? Since murder's so easy. All you need is a gallon of water, and the right amount of hate. You don't even need the water. And the hate, God knows, I had in abundance. Still have, still have. I water it daily, it's my only flower amidst this clatter of keys and concrete, I'll take it to heaven with me—that and my one good deed.

'Do you wish to receive the sacrament?' says the prison chaplain. Says it every week.

'What?'

I don't know why I say *what*, making him repeat his question with the same weary patience.

And I answer : 'No; my *hate* is my sacrament; my *hate*.'

Then comes his look of professional disappointment. 'I see no sign of repentence in you.'

'You're wrong,' I say. 'I repent not having murdered her sooner.'

This book would've gained, you'll be telling me, if I'd left all mention of the murder to the last few pages. But what point is there in my adopting a pattern of suspense when you've already seen my name on the cover? And what a memory you have! I'm (am I boring you?) 'the wife-murderer'. 'The' wife-murderer. Might it not help if you thought of me as an ordinary, good, imperfect human being? Forgive the snarl in my voice, but you speak of me as if I'd spent a whole life murdering wives. Instead of half an hour.

Twenty-seven minutes, to be mathematical about it. I timed myself. And even twenty-seven minutes, according to the Judge, was longer than necessary. The London media made capital out of it; capital letters, capital radio. The man in the street, that epicure of crime, thought I should be in for life. Because the public must be protected.

After all, I might remarry.

I'm the marrying sort. I must be. To have married *her*.

What's more I hated her from the start. Truly. This isn't the distortion of hindsight. I said to her: 'It's extraordinary. A few hours ago we hadn't even met, but already I feel more strongly about you than any other woman.'

And she grasped my meaning. For which I admired her. I must remember to say I admired her, lest you should dismiss me as quite mad. Which I most assuredly am not. You won't find me pleading insanity to you, any more than I did to the Judge.

'You're insane not to,' said my counsel, who had his reputation to think of.

Then it was some psychoanalyst's turn. Sick anal idiot. 'I can't think why you murdered her,' he said.

'Did you know my wife?'

The jury couldn't understand it. And yet, and yet, they understood only too well: they were married men.

True, they weren't married to my wife, nonetheless there was guilt in those headshakes. Making out they were shocked. Poor lady! A mother, too; devoted; because mothers, it would seem, are always devoted, particularly if you murder

15

them. You only have to murder them and they're instant saints.

She loved lawyers. Whereas I, oh yes, have learnt to hate them without exception or reserve. Insects peeping out of oakum, what stomachs they must have, that they aren't sickened by their own sweet unction.

If, mind you, I'd murdered some little schoolgirl, and schoolboy too while I was about it; murdered them and then raped them or raped them and then murdered them; if I'd skinned them, quartered them, sold them to Sainsbury's; in *that* case, you see, I'd have been mentally disturbed, an object of pity, needing treatment—care and after-care; but just because I murdered my *wife*, that, as these pricks would realise if they were honest with themselves, means I'm all too sane. Tell me, tell me a husband who hasn't killed his wife; killed her in fantasy after fantasy. Afraid to make fantasy a fact. Twelve men committing murder in their heart. But without the heart to do it. No heart. No guts. Hypocrites! Only sorry they couldn't bring back the rope, to hang their unfulfilled fantasies. Hang me for their fantasies. Hang me because their fantasies were unfulfilled.

Well, I'm in solitary confinement, isn't that enough for you? Or do you envy me that as well?

Perhaps you do. I used to long, year-long, to be alone. Years of fantasies! Yes, I too had my fantasies. She was late back, ten minutes late, had she fallen off an unfinished skyscraper, there're so many unfinished skyscrapers in London, surely she could fall off one of them?

Or under a bus. She was always threatening to. Ha! Did I say threatening? She seemed (quite seriously) to think I was incapable of getting on without her. Alone I was hopeless, she said; and I would never find anyone else to look after me in the way that she did. Then the sound of the key in the latch, I was in prison again, the only prison is marriage.

16

'Kill me,' she'd say. 'Why don't you kill me? You're not even man enough to put me out of my misery.'

'All right,' I said. 'I'll kill you.'

She told the child. 'Your father says he'll kill me.' So when I called at the house to take him out he couldn't come. He was afraid, you see, that's obvious.

Poor child! What was he to think? Believe? And when I disappeared out of his life for thirteen months, what then was he to think or believe? For it was thirteen whole months (I'm not exaggerating) between the party when the Bobby called and the Judge's hearing of my petition to see the child again. Her solicitors had brought an injunction against me.

And you should've seen her at the do where we first met : virgin smiles, straight out of school. The smiles, I mean. And she wouldn't say boo to the butter in her own melting mouth.

For thirteen months, child-months, he's forbidden to see me. And if his mother had had her way she'd have forbidden him for ever. Nor was she ashamed of telling her counsel so; or he of acting for her.

'First let me remind your lordship of how the Petitioner, with callous unconcern for . . .'

No, his lordship didn't need to be reminded, such was his disgust, no less, that a man of my standing—it wasn't as if I were some Welsh miner—should've behaved with total disregard for the child's welfare.

Bald, glabrous, pouchy-eyed, he looked in my direction, at me; and the intemperate manner in which he phrased himself was reflected in his eyes, his spectacles.

I looked back at him.

'You criminal!'

Not that I said it. I said nothing. But *You criminal!* was in my look, and that made do. His eyes, glasses, shone into anger; he (I could see it) was on the point of shouting at me, how dare I call him a criminal! But I hadn't spoken. It took

17

him a while (such was his anger) to realise I hadn't spoken, a quarter-second at the least. I'd (this once) kept to the rules, I'd remembered the important point, keep to the rules; because court isn't for discovering truth in: it's a stage, an ancient and venerable stage, where actors, remotely dressed, long exercised in court ritual, in all courtesy and courtliness, take their places on the differing level of an else-lost hierarchy, and (you think I exaggerate) enact a myth, oft sung to castle keep by bard and troubadour, wherein Woman, by nature good, is victim of base Man, from whom the Judge, a Knight (Judges are invariably Knights), is called upon to save her.

'As to the matter, m'lord, of the Petition, which you have heard from my Learned Friend, wherein the Plaintiff prays to be given resumed Rights of Access to the child of the marriage, I would stress that my Client, in whom Custody, Care and Control have been vested by the court, prays that the Petition be refused, such is her concern that the Plaintiff may otherwise be afforded further occasion of molesting her.'

'I'm aware how much this lady has had to endure, and she may be assured of my every sympathy, but I can hardly prevent the Petitioner from seeing the child altogether.'

'As your lordship pleases; but there's something I must bring to your lordship's attention. The child, during the period of the Petitioner's access to him, developed a twitch, which, m'lord, has disappeared since access was denied at your lordship's Injunction.'

'My child!' I said aloud—which was against the rules, I should've kept to the rules; that was my mistake all along.

And thou, respectable reader, if thou wilt live peaceably with the Law of thy Land, and offend not the Courts of thy Country; then, I counsel thee, love not the child of thy loins: for a Father's love delighteth not the Judgement Seat. There-

18

fore, I beseech thee, afflict not thy Soul if sickness overtaketh him, or danger threateneth; but lighten thy heart with indifference, and all shall be well.

Two or three months later I happened to meet his lordship at a reception in the Kensington Gardens Hotel.

'Good evening, my lord,' I said. Though he wasn't *my* lord. Lord of prejudice and ignorance. 'You may remember me. From the court.'

'Are you at the Bar?' he frowned, trying to place me.

'No, sir; but I've experienced you in your judicial capacity.'

'Ah. Not unpleasantly, I hope.'

'Unpleasantly? No no, I wouldn't say unpleasantly. But to *my* mind—and I speak as a layman—a comparison between Solomon and your lordship would not be entirely to the disfavour of Solomon.'

Dear God, the sweetness of my satisfaction when that anger reappeared in his eyes, his glasses!

He said: 'Your opinion is of no interest to me!' And added, rather illogically: 'Please explain yourself!'

Leave it at that. I should've left it at that.

But, 'If,' I said, 'in any other profession than the Law, you were to accept statements, totally unproven, and inadequately corroborated, as *fact*; you, my lord, would be fast finding your way into the ranks of the unemployed.'

His anger changed to a smile, for I was now attacking Judges in general, and he felt safe amidst their brotherhood. 'In the eyes of right-minded persons,' he said, 'vulgar abuse merits contemptuous dismissal.'

And he turned away in search of better company.

From my child, too, he had turned away: condemned him to more than a year of fatherlessness; and, on hearing my Petition, let him be with me on Saturdays, from two-thirty till five.

Two-thirty till five. So little time for doing; and none for

19

being. Was this better or worse than not at all? I scarcely knew. Or know. How can I balance the child's excitement at those afternoons against his bewilderment at their brevity? I had petitioned for the whole weekend, which was what he'd had before; but the Judge snapped at my Council for suggesting it. 'Certainly not!'

'Your lordship must pardon me; those were merely my Client's instructions.'

'Saturdays. Two-thirty till five.' He turned to my wife's Counsel. 'Are these hours convenient to your Client?'

Whispers.

'Yes, m'lord.'

'They are.' (Picking up his pen) 'Saturdays . . . two-thirty till five.'

He rose, we rose, he bowed, we bowed, he left by door at rear of stage.

But his anger remained about the court. And wasn't it justified?—seeing I've turned into a murderer?

I said to my solicitor: 'Will the child see me this coming Saturday?'

He nodded. 'The Order's been made.'

'Good. I thought it might take a few years to become operative.'

'No, no.'

'My wife, you'll have noticed, was always "this lady"; whereas I, unless I'm mistaken, was never "this gentleman." '

'No, you were "that man".'

It was meant as a parting witticism.

'There's presumably no point in trying the Court of Appeal.'

He made a face; shook his head. 'I think we have the best access we could hope for.'

And the Government will doubtless decide it came well within the terms of the social contract.

Lawyers! Why do they always say 'we'? The we-ing I was to endure over the months and years ahead! Have we committed adultery? (I beg your pardon?) We were to keep our adultery dark, he advised, especially the adultery we committed on the night of the child's birth, because that, quite frankly, wouldn't look at all good in a Court of Law; but we would have to admit it if we were cross-examined on that head.

'Saturdays, two-thirty till five. That's what the Judge said, didn't he?'

'Yes; I'll let you have the whole thing in writing.'

(More money.)

'What, in your opinion, is the reason for Judges always siding with the woman?'

'Well, you see, she's saddled with the child, so there's a tendency to try and rectify the balance.'

'Oh? How interesting.'

One learns. Had I not been to court, I would never've known that children are an affliction, which the estranged husband is fortunate to be rid of.

My poor wife!

CHAPTER II

Saturday, two-thirty, and I was waiting outside the house, rain pouring down. But I didn't take shelter in the entrance, gave no excuse for a second Injunction. Anyhow, the wet didn't matter, so long as my eyes were dry.

The door opened, my child was there, holding the handle, he still kept hold of the handle, it was higher than his head.

He wedged his foot in the door, pressed it wide with his body, let it close itself behind him. How tiny he was, I'd forgotten how tiny he was!

'Open your arms!' he said; and jumped at me from the top step.

'Now swing me!'

'My child!' I said.

'Go on!'

But the tears I'd kept out of my eyes, they sapped my strength, I could scarcely hold him.

'You've grown!' I said. 'How heavy you are! Let me put you down.'

But he wanted all the old games, just as if there had never been those thirteen months of not seeing me.

And in my bachelor bedsit it was the same : rocked on the gout-stool, blew open my broken pocket-watch, went through the boxes of indoor games before deciding which to play.

'I'm going to build a house in Park Lane.'

'I've built three in Lambeth.'

He shook his head. 'Mistake. Do you know why?'

'I will if you tell me.'

'Peppercorn rent.'

'You're wrong about Lambeth, you think it's just an archbishop and slums.'

'Concentrate.'

'Two-fifty a month.'

'Won't even pay for the petrol.'

'No?'

'Buy where the money is.'

'Get on.'

'It's your turn.'

'Oh.'

'Hard cheese.'

'Grasshoppers.'

'Throw.'

'All right.'

'All left.'

I threw. 'Five.'

'Go to jail.'

'Can't be.'

'I guessed.'

'Bank, change me a hundred for two fifties.'

'There.'

'Good boy.'

'What's the time?'

'Hour to go.'

'My turn.'

'Funny if you too landed up in jail.'

He clutched his head. 'I'm ruined, ruined!'

'Stop showing off!'

How convincingly he disguised his mockery as tragedy. Or was he disguising tragedy as mockery?

23

'Stop it!' I said.

He saw I meant it, switched to farce, made a Pakistani apology, hands at prayer, head bowed, backing to the door, I tried not to laugh, I couldn't help it, I laughed till I cried.

'You've made me cry.'

'I'm very-very sorry.'

'Did you pick that up at school?'

'Your turn.'

'Rent!'

'How much?'

'The house is yours, you should know.'

'Twenty-eight.'

'My turn.'

'Rent!'

'Too late.'

'No, it wasn't.'

'I'll pass it this time.'

'*RENT!*'

'Somehow I don't think that's very good for my ears.'

'Six.'

'Rent!'

'You're learning!'

'That was a double, I have a second throw, don't I?'

'Yes, yes, yes!'

'Don't hiss at me like that. Are you a cat or a steam-engine?'

'What's the time?'

'I've just told you.'

'What's the time?'

'Three fifty-eight and seven seconds.'

'Fuck!'

'*What* did you say?'

'Fudge. It's ancient Yiddish.'

'Like any with your tea?'

'Any what?'

'Fudge.'

'Yes.'

'Yes, *please*.'

'Yes, please.'

'Good boy. You have to add the "please", otherwise I haven't the faintest idea what you mean. Sugar?'

He took lump after lump, till the tea was up to the brim. 'I'll drink some, and then . . .'

'Would you perhaps prefer me to pour the tea into the sugar bowl?'

And then, quite casually, without warning, he said something I was to recall when murdering his mother : 'Why didn't you see me?'

I reached for the kettle, filled up the pot, then poured myself a cup. No milk. I've never liked milk in tea.

'These last thirteen months, you mean?'

'Yes.'

'Because I couldn't.'

'Yes, you could.'

What had his mother been telling him?

'You could,' he insisted. Then he dropped the subject, it suddenly seemed to lose his interest, he wore one of his Buddha silences, he could do it, same as my tenants, when I had them, but now no more, they might've been my children.

Poor tenants! Where're they now? I took my child back to North Kensington, past further evictions, from buildings they were used to, visually and muscularly. Why does the destruction so hurt me? Do I associate those condemned slums, that lend their darkness to the sky, with my own survival.

Under the new raised highway I pity those who're un-housed, un-apartmented. And, more, pity those who remain on either side—ear-split; community-split—till they too are evicted to make way for the kind of highrise where my child was soon to live.

'Well . . . goodbye,' I said, stooping to kiss him. 'See you in a week, all right?'

'No.'

'Why not?'

'It's a week minus two and a half hours.'

I laughed.

He didn't laugh back. 'Goodbye.'

'Good boy.'

He wasn't sorry to leave me; or scared of going back to his mother. As far as one could tell.

I walked away. In no particular direction. Where should I go? Back to my bedsit?

Guilt, suddenly. How could I leave him? Alone with her. She would do something to him, because the Judge had allowed me access.

Check he's all right.

Check? Don't play with your conscience. What use was *checking*? I knew what I should do, as if God had spoken. God *had* spoken: Take the child away—for good. Away, away, and build him a new house, with a new garden, in some new and undiscoverable world. Learn its language; and plants. Come naked; relying on mercy. Bring no glass beads, no, no. Or transistors. Or thermostatically-controlled refrigerators.

A church, it was open, you somehow expect churches to be shut.

I knelt on the edge of all that dark and damp, amidst musty missals, and the smell of yesterday's incense. 'Lord God,' I said; and my voice, it seemed, came to me from the far wall, spoke to me, 'if You're a father as you claim to be, take care of my child, don't let his mother hit him. I realise You may have other engagements, in which case comfort him

26

afterwards, first explaining who You are, because his mother doesn't talk about You. Say You're his Father in heaven, and remind him he has another father in the southern part of the Borough; and between us we'll do what we can for him.'

I went out again into the livid light of London; listened for the sound of smackings, as if I expected them to reverberate from one side of Kensington to the other. But no sound came. Perhaps she was getting his supper; reading him a story; helping him with his homework. She (in many ways, this was so astonishing) could be the ideal mother : stood no nonsense over food; saw he kept things tidy; taught the morality of please and thank you. And I often forgot this, which was bad; or, worse, though this I was rarely guilty of, let it lull me into unconcern.

That twitch! Why had he twitched when he'd had access to me? Because of his mother's smackings. Yes, but he had overcome it in those thirteen months of not seeing me. Had the smackings stopped too? Maybe—as long as she'd had her way. And would they resume?—till she went back to court, got another Injunction, because, m'lord, the child twitches as soon as he sees his father.

'But it's because she hits him, m'lord; I *know* because I've lived with her.'

'The child's been medically examined, there's no evidence to substantiate the Plaintiff's charge.'

With the flat of a hand, with the flat of a ruler. The mark's in the twitch.

I'm dreaming. The whole point about a court is that you're not allowed to speak. It's your Counsel that speaks. Speaks *for* you. Except that he won't, he won't say anything against the woman; that would be most ill advised, his lordship would lose patience if one said anything against the woman.

'But I've *seen* how she hits him, you haven't *seen* how she hits him.'

27

'She may have stopped.'

'And if the twitch returns?'

'It doesn't prove she's hit him.'

'Then why should he twitch? I do nothing to make him twitch.'

'He may feel torn.'

Torn! She *couldn't*. I would rather he was hit than torn. She wouldn't tear him. That's the ultimate wickedness. Enough that she hated me.

And why *why* this great hatred? Had I committed some crime unpardonable? Or did she hate me from the start? In which case, why had she married me? Some sort of need. She never said: 'I love you.' She said: 'I need you.' Why hate me, then? Because she needed me? She'd have preferred, doubtless, to build her blocks without me. But I was the mine in which she had to dig. She knew of no synthetic source.

Whereas I, thank you very much, could exist on my own, just about. Or marry someone else. *Any*one else. Except that it was her I fancied—which (let me waste no time in saying) seems utterly inexcusable, because I wasn't, after all, some savage, encountering the developed world for the first time. So why did I lust for this trinket?

'I need you,' she'd said.

But I never said I needed her too. And this (oh yes!) she resented from the start.

'Just because I'm a woman, that doesn't mean I'm going to honour and obey. You might not know it, being so old-fashioned, but honouring and obeying went out with waxed whiskers.'

She loathed me for the idea alone. And married me. What more effective punishment? Or more appropriate.

Teach me a lesson.

Well, I've learnt it, it's not in the curriculum, so I'll pass it on, it's this:

28

Woman is the active principle, man is the passive principle; woman is brightness, man is darkness; woman is artifice, man is nature. My ore (to me it was almost enough that it existed) to her was of no more than weekend value—until forged into some stronger, marketable product.

I first met her one April, quite by chance, at a reception for Friends of the Tate Gallery. (You probably know the word *friend*—spelt to rhyme with *fiend*, and pronounced to rhyme with *rend*, and meaning someone you can get money from.)

I'd been a Friend for years, I don't quite know why, having always kept clear of their functions, and I wouldn't have turned up now, except that I was at a particularly loose end, and thought I might cadge a glass of wine in return for all that 'friendship'. (It occurs to me, I've never cancelled my subscription, I wonder if I'm still paying it.)

Swing doors, the murmur of the crowd. Like nothing human; or even animal. It was the roar of breakers on distant rocks. Applause—like the vitreous crash of a cataract. And the dabs and blobs that we've come to interpret as faces.

Fuseli's fashionable fairies; the more exquisite for being diminutive; and the more repugnant. The sylphs that invade Pope's *Rape of the Lock*, floating above the satiric action like a rococo vault, only to reappear (have you forgotten?) as the bug Sporus.

Hard-edge. Art grovelling before technology. Inert Liquatex on the obligatory cotton duck—befetished with the bobs of criticism.

The people too were hard-edge. Conversation without give. Debate; without the risk of dialogue. People who knew about art; who talked about it; wrote about it; and for whom art did not exist.

The Tate is kind to April, for foxhunting is over, and the

London Season hasn't yet begun. You'll notice I use the present tense, but perhaps foxhunting and the London Season are things of the past, in jail one loses touch. But the flah-flah remains, I have no doubt: schools and the servant problem. Is it *still* schools and the servant problem? Can it *still* be? Well, at least they now have *me* to talk about.

Yes, surely you must remember him? Terribly tall. One never quite knew what he *was*. Sort of half-workman, half-playboy. Became a murderer. An occupation at last.

Oh, of course! It all comes back. Fingernails full of earth from potato-planting. They'll remember my homicidal quirks, my twitch, my give-away mannerisms; they'll remember them in the most conclusive detail, and all differently.

Some middle-aged woman with lambent eyes, born for this hour, was moving everyone around, lest there should be time for serious conversation. She felt my eyes on her, squeezed through to me.

'Would you like to join in the general conversation?'

But there *was* no general conversation. Only particular.

'I'd rather not, if you don't mind.'

She gave me a look of grave and temperate irony. 'Very well.'

Thank God I'm not a creative writer, condemned to sympathy! I have no sympathy with social grooming: men who've been to public schools and acquired the right faces; novelists, with their best work to come; the odd whizz-kid; a poof in pearls; young men who've written some of the most exciting poetry that no one ever reads; and what must've been the world's oldest hippy. Figures that summon no landscape, all joining in the general conversation.

For 'general' read 'light'.

Loneliness, I decided, is being among people who keep things light. Not among these do I find that handful of honest men to save the cities of the plain.

Knowing each other, they were excused from looking at the pictures. Many were related by marriage. More by divorce. All were terribly civilised. Civilisation, I should explain, means you're marvellous friends with your ex-spouse. My Lord Clark, my Lord Clark, what would you say if you were here? Perhaps you are.

I watch them surreptitiously helping themselves to the dip, as if it weren't meant for them. To the Saveloy sausages. And bits. Bits on bits. To the slices of egg with a black olive in the middle, like eyes, ugh! And when I think of my wife looking on me from her hard-edge afterworld, I see her with those egg-and-olive eyes, till I wish I could skewer them on a stick.

The women were worse than the men, the sort who complain about damp: doomed spinsters of forty, with spectacles on straps; and predatory divorcees.

Plainish, for the most part. Dowdyish; English.

And totally selfish.

Such women I'd fucked in my youth, and occasionally still did, taking them from behind with the impersonality of a beast.

But had never once loved.

I've loved a woman for her smallness, even for her bigness. I've loved a woman because she wears no bra, and needs none. I've loved a woman because she catches my joke, and the degree of joke.

Did I say *love*? No, not love. And yet, for this or that quality I've put women on momentary pedestals; yes, my past has enough pedestals to fill Crowther's in the North End Road. But if this wasn't love, it was something very like it: the same leap in the veins, which, even if you know it can't endure, none the less affords (like nothing else) a feel for the eternal.

We were to meet the finest painter alive in England today.

31

Really? It didn't say much for my careful coats of creosote on the garden fence.

Young women, pretty from behind. Some, indeed, were passable when they turned. And some were men.

Did I want a wife? Of casuals I'd had enough. Fucked every bint in Kensington; *and* her mother. I had hoped, was still hoping, though against all reason, that Miss Right would turn up. Against all reason, because I knew (had long known) that even when Miss Right did turn up, Mr Wrong had always got there first; and if by any chance he hadn't, this meant Miss Right wasn't really right after all.

And yet some woman of no oomph would probably, before the night, be added to my pile; meaningless, except as a monument to my own frustration.

Slip out. I wouldn't give a sneeze for any of them.

It was then that I noticed her, her eyes were a reluctant blue, her dress was white, shone, how hadn't I noticed her before? By the buffet. Blonde. Five-foot-nothing in high heels, hidden in the crowd.

I'm not trying to say I was in love at first sight. At first sight I felt hate. I mean what I say : hate. For I'm not confusing the first heart-pound with my at-long-last murder of her. No, I saw from the start that she had the Rialto in her soul.

But with the unimpassioned beauty of a miniature machine —exquisite in the economy of her shape, so that I longed, there, then, to undress her; did.

And felt the shrinking of my stomach.

She was with a man, her father; six foot, and iron. Thought he was God—and wore a beard to prove it. How, I wondered, had he fathered anything so delicate?

Rusted. Unwieldy.

And she so quick and new. An eye, electronic in its intelligence.

32

A man went up to her, I'd known him at school, an oaf, he was telling her a funny story and she laughed before he'd finished.

I liked that : laughing before he'd finished.

Lovely girl !

Her glance met mine.

Half-way.

Because she had the confidence of being blonde.

And yet I think I ought to tell you (though she didn't realise this) that the only women I love, or feel that love were possible with, are dark. Not merely because blondes tarnish. Blondes *do* tarnish. But (besides) they aren't right. Even their youth is wrong; there's nothing ancient about it.

She wasn't right. But somehow her not-rightness excited me.

Excited me. She knew. Unfortunately. Perhaps I should've done as the jade merchant does, who covers his eyes, lest they betray his enthusiasm for a piece of special beauty.

'Who are you?' I said.

'What do you do?' she replied.

It must be some fifteen years since this interchange took place, so I can't be sure of every word. Maybe we'd chatted for some time before I said, *Who are you?* And I don't suppose her *What do you do?* can have followed straight on.

But that's how I remember it.

'Do?' I said. Shrugged. 'Nothing in particular.'

She smiled. A woman's smile can mean *I want you*, or it can mean *Keep your distance*. It can mean *Stay*, or it can mean *Go*. But, with her—which?

'How very intriguing! Have you never . . .?'

'. . . I rowed for Oxford.'

She tossed her hair. 'My family haven't been to the university for generations.'

She spoke as if there were great merit in this.

I said : 'Do you come here often?'

'Life's so short,' she said.

We were silent for a while, I looked at the beauty of her, I found myself wanting to make it part of myself; and prayed that the barrier of words might not come between us.

Suddenly she frowned round, as if confronted by a hostile mob. 'I feel somebody's going to *spill* things on me.'

I suggested we tried the Turner Room. She smiled; she *hoped* I'd say that.

And she led the way, I marked the dilation of her *profil perdu*, she was still smiling, smiling back at me, pressing between the spinsters and the divorcees. Past whizz-kids, and the editor of *Witchcraft*.

Then she turned to me, another smile. Brilliance!

We were alone, in suggestive closeness, among the great academy concoctions.

'Turner!' she said. She said it so feelingly, as if it were more than a name.

A forumful of columns, sinking into earth, yet ready to heave a second time erect.

Storm over the Alps, a spatula of light, the Alps themselves a storm—as terrible as the seas in those last shipwrecks, where mountain-waves rise like fierce fish. A whole army, gowned in no known taste or time, spilling with seed-pearls, coiffed like priestesses, goes under. And so would you, if the sun were such an eye of retribution, dark, heavy and corporeal, as one day it will be, you'll find yourself caught, though I (and not you) am in prison, caught, all of you, I know it, in a chasm of thick light.

She moved closer to the canvas, peered among the spoils of Saguntum, gold and interior furnishings, sumptuous on rock and snow.

'I can't see Hannibal.'

'Of course not! *You* are Hannibal.'

34

'Aaah!'

She sounded . . . appreciative? Appreciative. Stood very close to me, so that her bosom touched my arm. And we were sucked into Turner's vortex.

'I think it must be the Brenner,' she said. 'Hannibal went over the Brenner. Do you know the Brenner? I was there last Easter. I remember it so well. I ran out of nail varnish remover; and couldn't think of the German for it.'

You see? She was like the others: the right amount of knowledge, the right amount of ignorance. But she did it better than the others, and that made it worse.

'I've never been abroad,' I said, refusing to play her game, but playing a game nonetheless, I hated myself for that, hated *her*. 'Except on a package to Paris. Loathed it. Left before the week was up.'

'Oh?'

Her voice was a little girl's; but her eyes, her pale blue eyes, had an unmistakable maturity, and I wondered, with something like fear, what had gone to the making of them.

'And to crown all, I was put on a bus for Orly, when I'd asked for Le Bourget.'

'On account of your accent?' she ventured.

Her jaw dropped a quarter-inch; and she left it there.

I saw her promoting men's cosmetics. And yet for a moment, unless she was the best of actresses, she had felt Turner's great encircling wave of pessimism.

I said: '(Do you know?) the next Ice Age has already started.'

'If it's already started,' she replied, 'it's not the next.'

I hated her. Did she realise that? Or was she only aware of having attracted me? She had attracted me. And for that I hated her the more.

I suggested our going out to dinner. She grinned, looking

35

up at me and making the most of my height. 'Yes,' she said, very simply.

'How about the Ghent?'

'Oh, lovely! I . . . don't think I know it.'

The Ghent would be lovely, though she didn't think she knew it.

CHAPTER III

'Two?' said the waiter, raising his fingers in a rude sign.

'Yes,' she said; and smiled at the décor, I *had* chosen well, you could be in Flanders, it was so Flemish as to be almost Japanese. The food, however, was the same as anywhere else—factory meat; and ye traditional olde soggie English vegetables. But it made no difference, our appetite was for each other, our voices touched in low candlelight, discussing North Sea gas, the disposal of difficult wastes, and the notorious needles experiment.

She brought the spoon very gingerly to her lips, as if tasting soup for the first time.

Smiled often; with the mouth slightly ajar. But in moments of concentration she would close in upon herself, like a clasp knife. Yet, either way, she was beautiful. Her very changes were themselves a beauty.

You now know how I surrendered to her inauthentic charm: life was *such* fun, sheer champagne, it went to her head, you could see it sparkling in her eyes. I admired her because she spoke of matters of concern. North Sea gas. The disposal of difficult wastes. And the notorious needles experiment. And they were of no concern because of the sparkle in her eyes.

'You're all that matters,' they said.

And her breasts heaved in one sigh of satisfaction—such full, firm breasts, there was a hardness about their softness, so that I yearned for her undressing; the unbuttoning of that shirt. (She wore no bra—just a plain and simple shirt, its beauty was what her breasts made it.)

Her nipples cast their own little shadows, which swayed in the candlelight.

(She knew it) she could madden the male, infuriate the female.

'It's as well I have a car,' she said; 'how do you manage without?'

'I take taxis.'

The very thought pained her. 'So expensive. Did you know cabbies earn £100 a week?'

'By God they earn it!'

'I wouldn't mind if they paid any income tax, but they're all on the fiddle.'

'Don't *you* ever fiddle?'

'I pay an accountant, that's different.'

I laughed. She laughed too. Her laugh said, 'How lovely my laugh is.' It was.

Then: 'Tell me where you live,' she enquired, almost as if she wanted to know.

'Near Ladbroke Grove.'

'Ladbroke Grove: off Holland Park Avenue; charming.'

'Ah,' I said, 'but you're talking about the *start* of Ladbroke Grove. Where James Pope-Hennessy lives. Actually it goes on and on for ever.'

'Like *The Mouse Trap*.'

'Or *War and Peace*.'

'Oh yes,' she said. '*War and Peace*. I'm afraid I never got further than the first few instalments.'

'Well, it ends with the retreat from Moscow. And so does Ladbroke Grove. Except that there *is* no retreat.'

She broke off a piece of bread and screwed it into a ball. 'So you go native in British North Kensington?'

'I'm African inside.'

She turned up her nose. Not that she had any colour prejudice. Quite obviously she was prepared to dislike blacks even if they were white.

And that reminded her: '*Hannibal Crossing the Alps* was painted, I believe, in eighteen hundred and . . . twelve.'

A slight pause before the *twelve*; the *twelve* was dwelt on, feelingly, you yourself felt the feel of that twelve as she rested her voice on it, as on a fur, the Tate was softened, its uncarpeted corneredness became the full roundness of her twelve.

Light that owed nothing to the shade. The shade itself a light. Darkened by the sun. I could've encircled her in my arms, all for the cookery of that one word *twelve*.

'But do go on about your house. *Is* it a house?'

'After a fashion.'

'Do you own the freehold?'

'What? Yes, I own the freehold. A poor thing but mine own.'

She ran both hands through her blonde hair, they held out the fineness of it, it seemed spun from the unravellings of a cobweb.

'*Is* it so very poor?'

'What can you expect? The rotten end of the Royal Borough.'

And then it occurred to me that she might not even know that the Royal Borough *had* a rotten end. So I added: 'You don't perhaps . . .'

'I *do* know. But . . .'

She didn't need to finish the sentence, the *But* was enough: Why did I live there? North Kensington is one of those overpopulated areas where *nobody* lives.

'You mustn't prejudge it,' I said. 'I don't suppose you've ever been north of the Park in your life.'

'Which street?' she enquired, just as if I hadn't spoken.

'Well, you know where . . . or rather you don't . . . where Ladbroke Grove meets Portobello Road, just above the Little Sisters of the Poor. Well, turn into Swinbrook Road . . .'

Her hand touched mine. "Not . . . It's Something House, isn't it?'

'Yes, Chivalry House.'

'Chivalry?'

She appealed for help, as if the word needed translating. 'You mean the stuff that isn't around any more?'

'Precisely.'

'Chivalry House,' she mused.

'How extraordinary you should know it!'

'It's my tiny dilettante mind.'

'But you've . . . past it?'

'More than once.'

'Strange I've never seen you.'

'Perhaps you don't spend your whole time looking out of the window.'

How incredible that of all the houses in North Kensington she should know mine! And I was also saying to myself, without any awareness of contradiction: *She must know all the houses in North Kensington.*

I laughed, she observed my laugh, the pleasure I took in her. 'To think that you, that *you*, should . . .'

'I help manage a property or two,' she explained very simply, as if they were wild flowers to be picked by the wayside.

Was it possible? This lovely girl! Apparatus of such exquisite economy. Functional as a 'fridge. Evolution stopped here. And yet the first amphibian to crawl out of the primeval slime would've crawled back if it'd known what I was to know.

Already knew. But never told myself.

40

'Come back for a drink,' she said. 'You must.'

The street swam in shadow. One last gash of sunset. And above shone an innocent young moon.

It noticed her.

Her car was on a meter, and that meter was different from all the other meters in the world.

We drove to South Kensington, the Royal Borough's Imperial end, with Indian railings and Roman porticos, a ghetto of the rich.

'You drive well,' I said. 'As soon as I saw you I imagined you behind a wheel. It's the alert look in your eye—as if judging whether there's room to overtake.'

About her body too there was something that told you she came from the same source as cars : the same compact power, the same unwasteful lines.

Ditto her flat. The antiques, though genuine enough, seemed straight from Rolls-Royce.

'Charming!' I said. And sank into its mink of condition. Not that I felt at home, home is for always, but now the now was enough, I was away from the unmade bed, forget the what-next.

'Do you like it?'

She looked vaguely about the room, apparently none of it had hitherto impinged on her consciousness. Then, suddenly returning to herself, she said : '*Will* you pour out the drinks? Men are always so much better at that sort of thing.'

She went over to the fire, poked it, put on more coal. 'And if you want to visit Queen Victoria, she's first on the left.'

Her voice had suddenly become soft. It was her soft voice. Attar of roses. She was trying it out on me for the first time.

And the last.

No, not the last. I heard it again when she said, shortly after we were married : 'I shall divorce you, you know. Not now. But I shall. In a few years.' Which she did. And a few years later still, I gave my best imitation of that voice of hers, saying : 'I shall murder you, you know. Not now. But I shall. In a few minutes.'

I hated her. Could've fucked her till she screamed. There'd have been (believe me) nothing artificial about her screams.

'Chivalry,' she said. 'Like knights of old.' And came at me with a glass, her fingers were right round it, I couldn't take it from her without touching her fingers.

What a limpid river she seemed! Later I was to know the chemicals in her, I was to pray she might go up in—as the Cuyahoga threatened to do—go up in flames.

And yet this role of innocence, however spurious in itself, seemed to suit her; seemed (without her knowing it) to be (in a way) genuine. I remember thinking so at the time, and wondering why. Perhaps because (this, I confess, has only just occurred to me) there *is* a certain innocence about the tribe she belonged to. The Hitlers, I mean. Worlds are their balloons, they play with them like children.

'When would you have liked to live?' she said, settling in front of the fire.

Was this a game? Her eyes said it was a game.

'I'd have liked to live after the Romans left, and before the Saxons came.'

She nodded very seriously. 'You should've been Boadicea,' she said with sad weariness, as if voicing a universally acknowledged fact.

'And destroy London?'

'Do help yourself. She was buried (did you know?) under Platform Three of Euston Station.'

'Who?' I said.

'Boadicea.'

'Boadicea! What brutes those Romans were!'

Her eyes shone in the firelight, shone like the lit lamps of a DS. Then dipped.

42

I asked myself how far one must return before arriving at civilisation. Had I been the burgher before he was bourgeois I'd have wanted to be the harvester before he sowed.

And this woman, if she had her way, would transform my *from* into *towards*.

She looked up, drew in a breath as if about to speak, then hesitated. Finally saying: 'Your compliment on my driving, I so appreciated it, I really did. Because I won't *tell* you how many times I failed the test, I nearly *despaired*. But something inside me said I had to go on, till finally it was the instructor who despaired: he passed me, poor man, because I was turning him into a nervous wreck.'

'Take off your clothes,' I said.

It only took a second to say; you see something from a car window, it's gone before you see it.

Her eyes widened. She sat very still. 'What?'

'You heard me. Take off your clothes.'

Her reaction was admirable. After all, we'd only just met, I might conceivably have been the sort you read about in newspapers. But she mustn't panic, her panic would only excite me, a woman's panic always excites the sort of man you read about in newspapers. Besides, she was calculating what to do.

I'm reminded of the day, all those years after, when I came to murder her. 'You're to be murdered,' I said. And I wasn't bluffing; she knew I wasn't bluffing. So, in a very businesslike way, computer-quick, she did the one thing that might've saved her. Admirable she was! Quite admirable! A shame to see her go. Not, mind you, that I'm sorry. It had to be done. Like bombing Zeiss.

'Take off your clothes,' I repeated.

She glanced at the door. At the phone, at the bronze table-lamp.

And then at the fire; the fire she'd poked and fed; it was

43

now crackling into flame. Yes, her one hope, as soon as I sprang, was the fire—to pick up a lighted coal in her bare hand, and thrust it in my face.

By the way, you mustn't think, just because of my eventually murdering her, that I have no sane desires; or that every time I meet a beautiful girl I order her to undress. I don't. Ask my acquaintances. If you don't know me, you're bound to know someone who does. (*Did*, I suppose I should say.)

For her, however, there was no asking around, not on that first night, alone in her flat, alone with a wild animal.

Six foot eight in bare feet.

I didn't spring, though. And still she eyed me. She eyed me. She had to. I might spring if she didn't.

'May I sit down?' I said, sitting down as I said it. 'Take your clothes off, it's something so simple, you do it every day. Why this lingering? Lingering means striptease, I'm not asking for a striptease, I don't want it, quite the reverse, you're to undress naturally, as if I weren't here. Except that I *am* here.'

'Are you mad?'

'Mad?'

Suddenly her fear had passed. Became anger. 'If you'd been mad I could've forgiven you.'

'Do you think I wanted to scare you?'

'No.'

'Well, then.'

'You wanted to *hurt* me.'

'How do you mean?'

'What I say.'

'*Hurt* you?'

'You should be ashamed.'

I shook my head. Why should I be ashamed?—when to undress was what she wanted. I knew it was what she wanted.

44

If it hadn't been for the wanting to she wouldn't have felt the hurt.

The same when I . . . you must forgive this emphasis on take-off and touch-down . . . when I came to murder her: 'You won't see me again,' I said. 'Good,' she said. I said: 'Take off your clothes.' 'Why?' she said. I said: 'Because I'm going to murder you.' The hurt in her eyes! Yet (isn't this strange?) death was something she wanted. Wanted to be dead, yet shrank from dying as if it were an immodesty. Such shrinking-from, and such wanting-to! Then the final satisfaction of realising she had no choice.

Like that first night: *Take off your clothes!* I said. There was now a difference in my voice. I don't mean an or-else, I don't mean a voice that said she was to take them off or I'd give her a little assistance of the kind she could do without; still less that I would beat her up or murder her. My voice, quite simply, gave her no possibility of refusal.

She couldn't undress, she was ashamed.

She would undress to make me feel ashamed.

Undress? No. She told herself quite firmly that she wouldn't; but her fingers moved though told not to, felt for the buttons of her blouse.

'Already?' she said.

Ah, I shall never forget that *already*. By God, *she* was seducing, she was seducing *me*, merely objected to the timing, the objection was part of the seduction.

I said: 'You make it sound as if we're total strangers. But we've known each other for hundreds of minutes, we've spoken tens of thousands of words. We've crossed mountains, commanded armies, feasted on ransom, felt storms, seen doom in the sun. And you say already! But what if we'd only met this moment? What if we hadn't said a word? Can't your form speak to me? What were we doing at the Tate if form can't speak?'

45

'All right,' she said. But half-fainting with shyness. And the blend of the shyness with the wanting to created the very striptease I'd told her to avoid. 'Be natural,' I'd said. But, one might argue, this striptease of hers *was* natural : she couldn't have undressed in any other way.

It was the nature of her unnaturalness.

And now, as I write, blot, write, in this senseless cell, what a world-apart that evening seems : the unbuttoned blouse, opening to cast a shadow on her breasts. Did I say shadow? A shadow is luminousness when a skin is like hers. Like a new gadget; and as simply geometrical, something you buy at the hardware counter, and called 'Roses in Milk'.

The falling of her hair to its full blonde length!

Then the stepping out of her skirt as if it were something she couldn't bear to part with, or as if the peeled-egg white-ness of her hips were a loathsomeness. Finally the careful unscrewing of her ear-rings, as if in that alone lay the whole of undressing.

Sat crouched on the carpet; an unvoiced call; simulacrum of perfection; tried to make a sphere of her nakedness, as if her body could be covered by her body.

I tore off my clothes as if they were a sudden torture. They were. I, too, could not have undressed in any other way. And I stretched down beside her on the hearth-rug, in the dark-bright light of the fire, myself a fire.

And around us lay silence, like deep snow.

(We'd not yet touched) for the first time I touched her, beginning at the ears, an adagio of petting, the anticipation and the moment.

My hand eased between her bosom and her thighs. 'Onto your back,' I said. And lay beside her, on her, felt her whole length, no, it wasn't *her* I felt, it was us, a new being, us.

My penis was a flame, aflame, her thighs were still to-

46

gether, my penis was licking against her thighs, as if into her, before into her. Then they opened.

And yet—you won't of course believe me—she (now; *now*) kept shut her cunt. Shut I tell you, tight, you don't think such things happen, it happened, this is no novel, it's Bible I tell you, she kept her cunt tight shut, its lips were content to nibble at the tip of me, to nibble-nibble, without any further discourse.

I grasped her ankles, thrust them round my neck.

'Get off!' she said. I raised my head, enough to see her eyes, they were cold, like chrome. 'Get off,' they said.

'What did you say?'

'Get off.'

Should I rape her? If you could call it rape. *She* would call it rape. It was rape, m'lord. I merely asked the prisoner back for a drink, did a perfectly straightforward striptease, petted him, opened my legs to him, and then, out of the blue, he tried to insert his penis in my vagina.

I mustn't do it, I'd feel sorry for the Judge, the maximum for rape is only three years.

'Get off!' she repeated.

'Please!' I said.

'*Please!*' she mimicked. 'You sound like a little boy.'

I got up, looked for my vest, it was somewhere inside my shirt. Said: 'I'll be going.'

'Please, Mummy, me wants pretty toy, will Mummy give pretty toy, please?'

I didn't answer.

'Little boy doesn't answer. You're a little boy, that's all.'

(Shrugging) 'Be that as it may,' I said. My voice was in-different, I could hear the indifference, it sounded like a voice from the next room, and I was glad of that, it was the only satisfaction I now had: my voice sounded like a voice from the next room.

47

I dressed. What for?

'Sulking,' she said. 'Little boy sulking. Just because he didn't get what he wanted.'

'Goodbye, then.'

'You've forgotten your underpants,' she said. 'I don't want you coming back.'

CHAPTER IV

Was it night outside? Or sick day. Silent, without whisper-music of grass or leaf; the street a howl of emptiness, receding to blue; not blue exactly, not a colour but a distance, a city without exit, as if space were time, and endless. But the endlessness held me in, I could scarcely breathe, the very air suffocated, and the final turning-to-blue of that milk-white stucco became the London fog of the foreigner's imagination.

The great portals of South Kensington rose up in sorrow, I wandered between them without aim, where could I go? Home? *What* home? With neither wife nor child, but only a burn about the genitals—for a woman I must learn to unmiss.

Stared down the perspective of entrances. I wanted to destroy all London—so that *she* could be destroyed. Didn't Shih Huang Ti burn all books, solely to obliterate any record of one woman's infamy? The fifth paragraph of the fourth chapter of the treatise Sanhedrin of the Mishnah declared that he who for God's sake kills one man destroys the world.

Bumped into a tree. Stopped. Leant up it for a while, leant up this lone suffering tree, asking myself what I hoped for, what I was doing, stuck on this cold star, where street-lamps exchanged yawns with the mist.

Neville Terrace, Carlyle Square, Glebe Place. Then a sudden glint like cutlery, is that the river? Thames, what you

49

could do if you tried! Rise from the male womb of the sea, rush upon London like some aged king. Drown that hard woman. Drown Kensington. Rise like some ancestral memory and break against the hills of Highgate and Highbury.

I felt faint; began wandering back, a stranger in my home town. It was a world I never made, was never made by.

Then suddenly Kensington South becomes Kensington North—a crumble of cornice and capital, the stucco of an earlier elegance, putrid, porous, pulverescent.

North Kensington! Animals shun it; bricks lose courage; only people endure.

If you can call them people. Yet I loved them, loved them more, perhaps, than I had ever loved anyone, or ever would. Until the coming of that child.

When my acquaintances talk about their attachment to the local people, they usually mean the policeman, or the baker you buy bread from. Whereas I, rather unusually for nowadays, had people of that class to live with me. I suppose they were what you would call lodgers, though I personally thought of them as tenants. And yet both words are misleading: 'lodgers' suggests that I gave them meals, which I didn't; and 'tenants' that they weren't in my own house, which they were.

I don't think I had ever said to myself, I shall take in lodgers. But one day (this was how it all started) I gave a lift to an old tramp in a collarless shirt, and took him back for the night.

He stayed fifteen years.

Stank.

Would I have stopped for him if I'd known he stank?

But he looked so solitary, standing there like the lone tree at Loos.

'Where're you going?' I said, tight-lipped, like a cunt.

'Nowhere in particular.'

Nowhere in particular. Such, it seemed, was his life.
Mine too.

'Well, in you get.'

He was bald and bearded, as if he had his head on upside down. No beauty; but with an under-handsomeness.

The car wasn't mine, I'd never owned a tin box in my life, was hiring it for a weekend. And I don't think I'd ever given a lift before, not in peacetime at any rate, but here was someone whose very back attracted me, what's more he had a limp, and snow lay deepening.

'North Kensington any good for you?'

'Good ride.'

'I dare say, but where will you sleep?'

'Rough.'

'Rough? But I thought there was a doss-house or something.'

'Was.'

'What?'

'Was.'

'You mean it's gone?'

'Council sold it.'

'Ah yes. If I remember rightly, they gave planning permission for a hotel.'

'Not another.'

'A council must be realistic,' I said; 'they have the rates to think of.'

'They want to get rid of us.'

'Us?'

'Us down-and-outs. They want to get rid of us.'

'And build hotels?'

'That's right. Hotels bring in the . . . what're they called?'

'Tourists.'

'No. The word you just used.'

'Rates?'

51

'Rates.'

I nodded contemplatively. 'Do you mind if I open the window?'

'Rather you didn't.'

'Oh. All right. Well, tell me, where're you going to sleep?'

'Rough.'

'Yes, but where?'

'Rough's rough.'

'Will here do?'

'Why, is this North Ken?'

'Almost.'

'Here'll do.'

So I braked, stopped, leant across, opened the door for him, gulped at the fresh air. 'Well, good night.'

'No loss, mind you.'

'What's no loss?'

'That place for down-and-outs.'

'Oh, really?'

'Do better under a bush.'

'If you can find one.'

'Funny world.'

'Yes. Well, good night.'

'Take car doors: they used to open on a back hinge.'

'I remember.'

'Before the war.'

'Yes.'

'Easier to get out.'

'Indeed!'

'And now they open on a front hinge.'

'Well, you got in, so presumably you can get out.'

'I just need time, that's all.'

'Look,' I said. 'I realise the weather's bad, but you can't spend the night in this car. For one thing, it's not mine, I hired it, and it has to go back.'

'I'm stuck. My leg.'

'What do you mean, *stuck?*'

'Stuck. Stuck is stuck.'

A sudden madness of fury rose inside me. 'You've had your lift, you old stinker, what more do you want?' And I got out, went round to his side, seized his ankle, wrenched it free of the door, tugged.

He was in agony. Good.

'Stop howling!' I said. Dug my heels in the snow, and (this if anything would do it) leant back with my whole huge weight.

But slipped, damn it! Fell back into the snow, the snow was in my eyes, up my nostrils. I had him, though; still had him about the ankle. I got up, brushed myself down, hoped no Bobby had seen.

Glove off, rubbing my eyes, I went back to the car, round to the driver's side, tripping over that foul old man's ankle, nearly fell a second time. Damn him! Let him lie there! He said he wanted to lie rough. Well, that was rough, wasn't it?

But (Lord God!) when I opened the door to get in, I found he was . . . still in the seat.

For a moment I—quite literally—lost consciousness. I'd given a lift to my Saviour, he had leprosy, that's why his leg had come off in my hands, I should've kissed him and now the Judgement.

I told you I was mad with fury, had I really gone mad? There weren't *two* of him, were there? One sitting in the car; one lying on the ground.

I must be careful, I must be careful, snow can do strange things, it can beckon the exhausted to its white pillow, whisper that all will be well if only you lie down on her. Can it tell me that the tramp I'd just tugged onto the pavement was still moaning in the car?

I'd have seized him again, by the shoulders this time, except for that moaning.

'What's the *matter?*' I said.

He lifted up the skirt of his coat. One leg was missing. The leg that had jammed.

'Where's it gone?' I said. 'Have I . . . pulled it off?'

He sobbed, sobbed, old man's sobs. 'I'll never get another. They charge you. Second time round they charge you.'

In such pain, such pain, and thinking about lack of money, or perhaps the lack of money was the pain, I don't know, I felt such sorrow and self-hate, the unnecessariness, why had I done it?'

I got out and fetched the leg, the bits of broken straps, held them as if they were a child, as if they were a child of mine, as if they were the tramp himself, as if the tramp were my child.

And yet, if I'd *had* a child, would I have been so angry with this poor old man? Did I punish him because I had no child? I think I punished him because I had no child.

Poor old man, he had no child either.

I kissed him. Maybe you admire me for this. Don't. My revulsion had quite past, I couldn't have felt less revulsion if he'd been one of the wingless angels of Michael Angelo.

And I would've asked him where he lived and driven him home, I would've driven him home if he'd lived in Perth; but he had no home to go to, not even a childless one; not even a Home. So I took him home.

Still sobbing, he searched for his one handkerchief, it was stained with the snot of years.

I put an arm round his shoulders, and another round his one leg; carried him; with all pity and love, and with perhaps a thought that if I left him he would report me to the police.

Over the spalled pavement, the crunch of snow, the snap

54

of gelatinous ice. In at the back door and up to what was called the spare room, though in fact most of the rooms were spare.

Phew, the weight of him! But I'd managed it, my arms're like other people's legs.

'I'll run you a bath, can you get into a bath with one leg, I'll help you. And let me have your clothes, you can borrow some of mine, keep them if you like, they'll be big, though.'

'Right you are.'

'And wash yourself properly, hair included, my cat'll teach you, I don't mind a bit of stink, but you overdo it.'

I could never have got him a job, what with his age and one leg, so next morning I showed him the garden and asked him if he'd like to help me.

'Nice bit of dirt,' he said, shaking his head as if to dispel any doubt on the subject.

'And that's my cat.'

'Go on.'

(It suddenly occurred to me) my other empty rooms could be filled too. I put a postcard in the local shop. Let to . . . not down-and-outs, but lonely nonetheless; charged rent, they couldn't all be my gardeners.

I said they weren't down-and-outs, but they all (in some way) seemed down; and out too. Out because their landlords had wanted to improve, you improve with an Improvement Grant from the Kensington Borough Council; because Kensington Borough Council wants better housing that's within the means of better people. So the landlord's helped to convert ten lousy bedsits into three luxury flats, that the Scriptures might be fulfilled : To him that hath shall be given, and from him that hath not shall be taken away even that which he hath.

Including his lousy bedsit.

Without the offer of alternative accommodation.

But not to worry, the area improves. The Council, don't forget, is in business, it has to balance its books, so don't blame the Council.

I can't tell you the number of my tenants in that unmarried time. But they were all lonely—either lonely and brave, or lonely and self-pitying. And the self-pitying were the loneliest, because self-pity drives out pity.

Life distorted; wrenched, mutilated; perverted away. Some of them were chatterboxes; but most remained so fast in their boxes that nothing could lever them out.

'Care for a cup of tea? And a biscuit?'

(I'm thinking of one in particular. Youngish.) He would hesitate, as if waiting for himself to speak.

'Never say no.'

He lay there in the tenseness of no touch, consoled only by the feel of darkness, which was nature to him, I saw it with his eyes, while the chinks of day where the curtains failed to meet had the crudity of artificial things, interfering with TV.

I had at first wanted to turn it off, the TV I mean, draw back the curtains. Perhaps he was unaware that it turned off, curtains drew back. But he wouldn't have thanked me, because TV protected him, assured him that nothing would happen, because things went on; and the drawn curtains were his escape, his escape was never-go-out, there *was* no out.

'You ought to get up, go out,' I said.

He dunked his biscuit, hesitated, as if the giving of an answer were more than he could afford.

'There's no ought,' he said. He knew a landlord couldn't make him go out, a landlord could only make him leave. Would he yet again have to leave? He looked anxiously at his one suitcase, from which, torn at the seam, clothes spilt like entrails.

56

I said: 'There's no need to go. You can stay here as long as you like.'

He lived, was, a still-life. So secretive, secretless, in his one-room world.

'And you don't have to get up if you don't want to,' I added. What had he to get up for? Had he anywhere to go that was half so beautiful as bed?

Why not sit? No, you get cold if you sit, you have to put a sixpence in the meter, he had no sixpence for the meter. Anyhow, with sitting you get so bored, bored. He'd have had to tidy the room before he could reach a chair, and on his one chair was the suitcase, he'd have had to move the suitcase, but where to?

I also had a man with a dog, no other landlord would take him because of his dog, he couldn't live without his dog.

'Does it bite?' I said.

He looked at it, as if to make sure it wasn't listening. 'Only in play.'

'I see.'

'He never *means* it.'

'It's the thought that counts.'

'Man's best friend.'

And my cat surveyed its landscape of smells.

I had an ex-sergeant of thirty years' service, he wore the Africa Star, it was the medal he felt proudest of. But his reminiscences were never about fighting. Only dust. And not the dust of the desert but the dust of the barrack room: a thirty years' war against the dust in the barrack room. He continually re-arranged the ornaments on his mantelpiece, but without achieving any perceptible improvement. The magnifying glass he so laboriously polished was already clean. He wound up his watch several times an hour and glanced at it so often that the time no longer seemed to register. One day I went into his room and found him standing on a chair which he'd placed on the table. 'Dusty cornice!' he said, showing me his finger. One day he was dusting the light-bulb on the landing when he got giddy and fell down the stairwell and died—died, you might say, fighting the enemy.

I only had one woman, she charred for me, thirty-five, and her teeth in a glass. Not seldom she opened her door wearing only a petticoat; not to attract, but because she was sure she couldn't. Chain-smoked; using her cupped palm as an ashtray; she never gave it up, her nerves were something shocking, what with all this scare about cancer.

I had a Turk who once kissed me on both cheeks and told me he loved me. To my eternal shame (I merit prison for this alone) I hesitated a whole moment before I could bring myself to reply, 'I love you too.'

And I did. I loved all my tenants.

Therefore, when mischief-makers, who justified themselves under some political name, such as Peace Party, slipped slogans through my door, setting tenants against their landlord, I felt as if nature itself were attacked. Would you set children against their father?

Most, I loved the one-legged tramp. I taught him to read; and sometimes, looking in through his window, I would see him over a book, poring with such still appetite, as if listening to the words. I felt so humbled by his dignity, and was never tempted to smile if (right to the end) his lips moved at the syllables, or if he never aspired beyond children's war comics. In fact I was almost relieved, because I can tell you that the tenants who read the best books are invariably the lyingest, light-fingeredest and rent-defaultingest of any. I'm not trying to make a point out of this, I'm just saying it's so.

He made no friends besides myself; and the wage spiral was a party he never thought of being invited to. But he gardened well, if slowly. Read slowly too—you would think one leg of his mind was missing. Old age. Or perhaps he had never heard of hurry. If he had, my house allowed him to forget it. At any rate, his pace was always the same limping andante—as if he knew he was immortal; or knew he wasn't.

(I'm not exaggerating) he was my dearest friend; *is*. Dead for years; but I think about him a great deal, and I hope he thinks about me too.

Lodgers came and stayed; or came and went. But there's no point in describing them all, they were so alike, they had their isolation in common. Each of their sentences began with 'I'. Not the 'I' of Cartesian plenitude, but the 'I' of isolation. Curtains drawn (I think I've already said this), as if daylight were some fearful artifice. Keep life dark: darken the sad snapshot on the mantelpiece, with its attempt at a smile, the attempt to forget pain, only more painful. The never going out, the staying with marinade, furred-up kettle, brunch and high tea. Staying in bed. Such cautious lives, if you can call them lives. Nothing ventured, nothing lost. Alone with their tics, the repetitive thumb-twiddling. Give them a rocking-chair and they'll rock all day, rock at a body-beat. How, if I were to describe them, could I distinguish between one and another?—between those who did absolutely nothing, and those who did nothing absolutely.

What contact could I really have with them, though they had the need to talk? The need to say something, though they had nothing to say.

'Have you the right time?'

Why do the lower classes always say *right* time?

They valued my calling on them; knew, though they might live alone, that they would not die alone.

I can't recall how I got led into talking about my tenants. I was returning from that little blonde's flat. Returning to my tenants, ah, that was it. Needing them as never before, and determined to love them more than ever, so that I could make up my mind never to see that evening's nakedness again.

59

What if she *was* a perfect beauty? So is the Marble Arch—which leads from nowhere to nowhere.

But night came, and brother ass, my body, eeyawed for that little fairy queen—touched her exquisiteness with a tender dread, from the delicate Arab arch of her feet to the grace that sat on her head like the crest of a peacock.

In such manner may love come upon my enemies.

CHAPTER V

And next morning—I'd already willed the telephone to ring—she rang. 'It's *me*,' she said, as if there were no one in the world I'd rather speak to.

'What do you want?' I said. Have no further commerce with her.

She was silent.

Finally she said : 'I want you to apologise, that's all.'

(To apologise.)

'It's the least you can do,' she added.

What reply would you have given?

'You should be a Judge,' I said. Punish the victims, demand apologies from the insulted. (No, on second thoughts I didn't say that : as yet I'd endured very little law.)

'I'm coming straight over,' she said; 'you can apologise to my face.'

'I don't remember inviting you,' I said.

She'd be round in ten minutes. Was.

And (incredibly) I'd be opening the door to her as soon as I heard the gate. Because lonely. All *from* : no grasp of *to*. Escaping without map or compass.

She grinned. 'Do you mind lowering the drawbridge?'

'You're beautiful!'

'Had you forgotten?'

'You're different : you've exchanged the beauty of the evening for that other beauty of the morning.'

'You don't object to my wearing trousers?'

She was dressed for North Kensington—almost, one might say, for the North; yet she obviously came from the South, you could tell from the lustre of her eyes.

'Come in.'

She glanced round the hall and the stairwell, her frown was asking how I could *live* here, and I began asking myself the same question, how *could* I live here?—with neither the responsibility of the married man, nor the discipline of the monk.

'Do you have *any*one?' she enquired.

'What?'

'To look after you.'

'A daily. Or twice-weekly, rather. Did you hear a glass breaking? That's her.'

'Ah.'

Those eyes said North Kensington's filthy; spoke of the Borough's butt end as if it were one big rubbish tip.

I said with a vague wave : 'These streets're condemned by the Council.'

She nodded. 'Condemned because condemned.'

'Ah, how true!' I said, as if adding a new thought.

And how admirable!—that she should know these things. Care. Care enough to know. What meaning, after all, could North Kensington have for her? Here were no Ritz or Rolls, no Sealyhams, no Brie, no pre-preparatories; not even a Sainsbury's, or Church of Christ Scientist. But a barren poverty had wiped its arse over every ward. North Kensington would never be designated a conservation area, because so little was left to conserve. It's terrible the way people neglect their property when it's scheduled for redevelopment.

She surveyed the cornice. It was flaking.

I said : 'Let's sit down in the drawing-room. Make yourself at home. Just don't tread on the cat.'

'What *is* it about North Kensington?' she said, sighing onto a sofa. 'I feel dust in the throat.'

'Well, have a drink. Whisky?'

She was silent for a second. 'Provided there's any water.'

'Will the tap do?'

'If it's safe to drink.'

'It's safe enough. Just tastes horrid, that's all.'

'Such a bore to boil it.'

'But be careful not to breathe the air.'

Her eyes widened into mock-surprise. '*Is* there any?'

I laughed. 'Not if my tenants had their way.'

'Oh, tenants!' she exclaimed. And her eyes narrowed into anger. *Real* anger. 'Tenants're vermin.'

I wasn't shocked. I knew what she meant. 'It's as well I keep a cat, then. On the rocks?'

'Yes, please.'

I went into the kitchen, opened the fridge, pulled out the ice-tray and took it to the sink, holding it under the cold tap.

She said: 'What's wrong with the hot? Afraid the ice'll squeal?'

I murdered her; it was what Jesus would call murder. I wished her dead.

'To come back to your tenants,' she frowned. 'Surely you don't have them under your very *roof*?'

'Yes, I do.'

'Tenants under the roof. How *could* you?'

'They're the poor lost tribe of Israel.'

She snorted. 'I can understand why God never troubled to find them.'

I thought of their eyes—eyes like pit ponies. 'I love them.'

'*Love* them?'

'Yes,' I said. And added with deliberate pomposity: 'This may be an error, but it's one I don't intend to rectify.'

'Why such animosity against all that's happy and harmonious?'

For a moment I thought she was speaking of herself. But she added: 'They're so *ugly*.'

'Tenants?'

'Ugh!'

She would never realise: what she called an ugly person was a beauty she hadn't looked at long enough.

I said: 'What you call an ugly person is a beauty you haven't looked at long enough.'

'Life's so short,' she sighed.

'Short of love.'

'So you let rooms.'

'Just about.'

'And pretend you're a Victorian *paterfamilias*.'

I hated her. With all my heart. Till hatred became desire. I hated that too.

Near, I looked at her eyes—how they closed; and how they opened. There was a grasp in the closing of her eyes; and in the opening of them. She'd be aware of my seeing their closedness; and she opened them to meet mine.

Touch her. Not to touch her was an agony.

'Would you mind moving away?' she said. 'To let me breathe.'

'I want to touch you,' I said. 'To the very heart.'

As if she hadn't heard, she said: 'When're you going to apologise?'

I shrugged. 'Now, if you like.'

'Apologise, then.'

'I apologise.'

'You worm!'

'Feel better?'

'No.'

'Last night—do you realise?—I hoped the Thames would

inundate all London. Completely. From Claygate to Noak Hill.'

'How charming! Just to drown *me*.'

'Oh, I grant there's a more economical way of doing it.'

'You haven't the guts.'

'How do you know?'

'I'm still alive.'

'It's the thought that counts.'

She drained the whisky from her glass. 'Presumably your mad mind said I *was* London.'

I looked. If I looked long enough she'd be ugly. But (my child!) I *didn't* look long enough, a few years would've done, and my body refused to wait that long.

So the stairs were an embrace about us.

You'll say I loved her. No, it wasn't love. But it was fierce enough, a heat in the belly, while my head remained cold. Heat! But I was above it, the waves never reached *me*, I was above them, they were on the floor below.

If only sex were a solitaire, not this game-for-two, if only you could do-it-yourself. Had it not been for . . . No, what's the use? Stop the if-only. Sex (we weren't touching) was the space between us, it was around us, we were standing within a field of force.

And the bathwater ran from the geyser, warming the walls.

She took off her shoes, as if to make herself smaller still; and with no tongue except her eyes, watched up my lips for me. Yet all my lust was somehow centred on her feet.

I took off my own shoes, and socks, and placed my toes on her insteps, we were so near, and yet (except for those feet) not touching, as if it were against the rules of some child-hood game.

Then I undressed, while she, from the ankles upward, was still quite clothed; I undressed completely, without unzipping a zip of her; so near that she must almost have felt me, could hardly have seen me—except the eyes, we looked into each other's eyes, because eyes, being naked, are therefore not naked.

She looked into my eyes so as not to look at my nakedness, and I looked into hers because they were the naked part of her—if not the whole of her : the being exposed.

She too undressed, going through the motions with ceremonious nonchalance.

And then—the first touching of hands—as if our previous encounter had never been.

'I desire you,' I said.

She knew it was a way of saying I didn't love her.

I desired sex in the bath, and the bath itself was sex. The touch of another skin is too particular except in the context of water's all-round warmth.

I was over her. No more than my breathing pressed on her. She lay quite still; like a sacrifice; neither accepting nor rejecting. But at the first feel of my penis she tensed, and her very walls shuddered, why this fear? 'It's all right,' I said; 'a penis is only earth, not a sword.'

It was a sword : you could feel from her body, see from her face.

Then suddenly it dawned on me, a reddening, a reddening of the water, clear as any sunrise, like a myth of battle.

She lay back, as if wounded, dead, I felt tender and annoyed, there was a rim about her throat.

I got up, out, stumbled over her shoes, those detestable little shoes like mousetraps. 'Why didn't you tell me?' Imagine it! For more than twenty years she'd been a martyr to purity.

Her glare! '*Tell* you?'

'I thought—'

'You *didn't* think. That's the whole trouble.'

She gave a dry laugh, it rang without resonance, I hated

it, it was a handful of small change, flung down. And her body of such uncanny loveliness, like something that had happened elsewhere.

Blood and water, I would have licked it from her if she'd returned me any tenderness. And have drunk it from the bath.

She reached for the plug, pulled it out as if the water were her anger, and she wanted to release it.

A glurg. The bath and the basin were drawing on each other.

'I'm going home,' she said.

'Don't let me keep you.'

'Throw me out. Typical.'

I waved her car goodbye. My hand felt like a separate thing.

And my feet wouldn't return me to the house, I sensed it was no longer mine, but a blueprint in *her brain*.

I turned to my plants, asked them to cultivate me, together we could win.

But I never listened to them; told myself she was shy. (Why are the middle classes never rude? Only shy.)

Shy! What if I tell you she (within weeks, *days*) was calling *me* the virgin; me!—who even shunned the latest super-loos, because they showed up my poor worn prick.

Shy! She! Came back that very night, wearing nothing but a fur coat and her damned mousetrap shoes, 'Can I take my coat off?'

I'm not trying to shock you. I don't suppose you're shocked. You're not even surprised. You've read the latest novels, you can claim you aren't surprised by anything at all. Not even a woman's quick-change. Quick-change is what life's all about, it's as commonplace as childbirth, as unremarkable as dawn. Why should you be surprised? Does it surprise you, for instance, that a subordinate star, after aeons

67

of inescapable and insufferable light, should've darkened to earth? At the beginning of this century the fastest means of transport was a horse; and now you can reach the jungle in an hour. None of this surprises you, so you won't be surprised, either, if I tell you how this girl, who yesterday had shrunk from a penis, was soon wide open to me, as if she wanted to turn herself inside out.

She *did* turn herself inside out : her shamelessness was the inside-out of shame.

CHAPTER VI

Milk bottle tops. Cars that won't start. Blacks with their fatal foreignness, their helpless ventriloquism—in curtainless basements, fetid, rank, labyrinthine, where sanitation means a pit, and their only warmth is in their frozen fryings.

A sun hung above the fumes, a sun without rays, tin, looking as if it had lost the earth, lost it and lost interest in it. Because, you see, the sun is for the South; and South Kensington. And what did this land of flaked plaster have to do with South Kensington? No link except the passing buses. Does your butcher sell jewellery? Harrods.

And that girl, who I'd best chuck.

The cry of the paraffin man was coming round the corner, his cart clattering over the rough road, seemingly set in motion by the roughness of the road. I must catch him, he sold me his horse's manure, box-loads, and the soil of North Kensington needs it; the real thing, not like those sackfuls that peddlers try to palm you off with, all mixed with straw. 'Paraffin' he cried—except that the decades had pared it down to a sad 'Aaah, eee!' A bell, and 'Aaah, eee!'

My body too cried a sad *aaah eee*, reminding me that I'd fucked, and wanted to.

Diesel oil. The dry gargle of a two-stroke engine.

Loneliness! I didn't say to myself, *I am lonely*. I went into the garden and talked to my plants—knowing that they see though eyeless, and hear though earless.

And then I'd go and talk to my other plants, those indoor plants, my tenants. I knocked on the door, though knocking was a formality : they could never hear with the TV on. And they never turned it off, they let you shout against it, they didn't seem to know that it *could* turn off.

My old gardener. Not that he gardened any more, but he still spoke to the plants, which is a *kind* of gardening; kind indeed. I liked his way of speaking; the words were there before they were spoken; speech was a mere darkening.

I pass to the next tenant, 'Good afternoon,' never an answer, beyond an almost imperceptible nod, as if bidding at auction. A man no older than myself, but lying there, not ill, waiting lifelong for death, in the posture of death.

On the bed a caged hamster, always running in his wheel. For pure exercise? Or to escape?

And then a homo with a sympathetic manner, ex-seller of ties, he was always pleased to see me. 'Hello *sir*.'

'I mustn't stay.'

'No, of course not, out with a young lady, you're much in demand, I'm sure.'

'I don't know about that.'

'Well, *have* a nice time,' he pleaded. Adding confidentially: 'And take my advice, don't stay sober : it's not worth it.'

'No, you feel so dreadful next day.'

Dear gentle person. And now that I'm in jail I expect he's still all sympathy—he knows I wouldn't murder without cause.

To be rid of the tenants, that's what my little blonde had made me long for. Rid of the furred-up kettle; spider-thin counterpane; wash-bowl with dirt-rings that no scouring would remove. I'd had enough of unmade beds, gravy-coloured carpets, and brick that's uric at the joints, pitted as if a plague had passed. What was I doing here? In the throw-away, take-away, motorway end of Kensington. The While-U-Wait end. Keys cut—While-U-Wait. Windscreens fitted—While-U-Wait. By God, U-Wait! It's the District of Waiting—till the waiting becomes a kind of Pharaonic stagnation.

It was now dark. The houses seemed higher, closer together, they cast their darkness upward, it was getting into my eyes, till I felt trapped, sunk out of the given world. Yet unable to escape, because I had to stay for my tenants, I had to stay so that they could stay. 'You can stay,' I'd promised them. But now? Was I to lose my life for them? And yet, why save it, if, in so doing, I lost what I lived for? I lived for my tenants, didn't I?

Or for that woman. If you could call her woman. Ah, but *yes*, that was the whole hurt of it all, she *was* a woman, she was a *woman*. Swear never to see her again.

But my penis swore back, a trooper riding me, flush-faced and naked to the spurs. Had me round to her apartment.

'You're mad,' she said.

'I'm mad about *you*,' I said. Mad to say it.

'That's just the point, you're not.'

'Then why the hell do you think I'm here?'

'I can imagine,' she snorted.

I tried putting my arm round her, it was like putting an arm round a board.

She said: 'Wouldn't you by any chance think of asking me what I *do*?'

'I'm interested in what you *are*.'

'It's much the same thing.'

'Well, I already know what you are, so that's all right.'

Except that it wasn't all right.

'It *isn't* all right,' she said. 'I have my own life to lead.'

'What do you do?'

Her eyes scraped about in mine for any trace of mockery. She then said: 'I work for Bethell.' But she didn't really *say* it, it was as if her voice had written it, like an entry on a

71

form. And added: 'I'm secretary to the Managing Director.'

'Oh? I can guess who manages who.'

'Care to stay for supper?'

'Yes, please.'

'Take pot luck.'

'Pot?'

She was silent, the words weren't bringing us together, they were the beginning of our long division. And I think she realised it, because she suddenly burst into tears, she would try tears as an alternative, I think I was moved, or maybe just surprised. Somehow shocked.

I wanted to take her in my arms, but she, no longer crying, very abruptly said: 'Look, where's this leading?' And her voice seemed to bar the way.

'Leading?' I frowned. 'Is it a road we're on?'

'Well, quite, *is* it? That's what I want to know. Don't get me wrong, I'm not *proposing* to you or whatever, I wouldn't *propose*. I just . . . Do you intend to marry me or don't you?'

The answer should've been so simple, but the hour was late, she might be the last bus, she wasn't really travelling in the right direction (I knew it), nonetheless I'd better take her, I was afraid of being left at the stop when everyone else had gone.

'Marry me,' I said. 'Marry me, do. You must. I can't think past you.'

But the trouble was that I did think past her, I was thinking of the child, in a year we'd have a child.

Except that I *wasn't* thinking of the child.

'Will you?' I said.

'If you're keen,' she said. And she laid her head in my lap. There was a conscious elegance about the laying of her head in my lap.

I said: 'It'll mean living in North Kensington.'

Only after some seconds did she answer, as if North

Kensington were very far away, and her mind needed time to reach it. 'All right. Get the workmen in.'

She made love with me—on top (this was the place for her, I should've thought of it myself), her vagina capping the head of my penis, trying it for size, but so cautious, like answering the door at night.

But each time she was bigger, till she seemed to swallow me whole.

CHAPTER VII

Here comes the bride. A church wedding, the first for both of us, it might work, you never know, beginners' luck. But what a performance! So much organ for such a diminutive figure, an elephant seeking its young.

Figurine. You could hold her in one hand, I wanted to hold her in one hand. But as she approached up the aisle, between hats the size of table-tops, her slenderness (more and more) towered. My eyes, beginning at her feet, felt they could never lift themselves high enough to reach her head. Would my house be too low? Would the workmen have to start again? Yes, this was it, the workmen would have to start again.

To think about workmen at my wedding! But when it came, it seemed to come without warning. In spite of those weeks of preparation, it caught me in mid-commonplaceness. In fact I'd just been having a word with my tenants, they were about the only people on my side of the church. About the only people on my side.

'Yes, do invite your tenants, it'll be fun.'

She didn't mean it'd be fun for *them*, and it wasn't, they looked as if they'd passed through the wrong door.

'You live in the big house,' she assured me, 'so it'll be all right.'

She may even have hoped they would touch their caps—

though, as no one knew better than herself, tenants're all too liable to make other gestures nowadays.

'As long as they sit at the back,' she said.

The organ was declaring that things had approached the finality of a beginning. She, tiny again, was now at my side, a light against the darkness of my morning coat. Could this be the marriage of opposites in which Heraclitus saw harmony? So beautiful she was, I could've fallen for her, fallen, fallen, nearer, my God, to Thee.

Assured because all that white was without spot or wrinkle, I stared at her till my eyes failed with longing. Whereupon the parson required and charged me if I knew any impediment. 'Yes,' I replied. But only to myself. Only to myself— and that, *that* is what I shall have to answer for at the dreadful day of judgement, when the secrets of all hearts shall be disclosed.

'The ring, given and received, is a token and pledge.'

Suddenly I was in love. Or was I only in love with the words?—those words whose every syllable was uttered in a certain way, else it would've lost its power to ensure the numen did its bidding.

'Let us pray,' he said, which is parsonese for *Now kneel down*. And it was time to say *I do*, I should've said *I do* when he asked me if I knew of any impediment, but now I was married, though hanging were cheaper. 'Till death us do part,' he said. And I knew this was no cant.

He raised his hand in blessing. Beamed. 'Would the bride care to sign the register?'

'If it makes you happy,' she said.

Music, the kind called sacred.

We turned. The eyes of the congregation were on my bride, except for an occasional glance at the bridegroom, who was by no means without spot or wrinkle.

She looked as sweet as if a cloud would hold her, all white

in the noonday, like Venus and Victory. But why, in God's name, had she married such an old man? He seemed older than old; older than man. And he wasn't even *somebody*. They'd have understood if he'd been *somebody*.

The wedding march from *A Midsummer Night's Dream*. Titania and Bottom, we walked (what were they thinking?) down the aisle. But it wasn't walking, it was a representation of walking. We passed through the smiles, but they weren't smiles, they were mimes of smiles, smiles that bet the distance between the church and that little paragraph in the gossip column which would say we were good friends.

(Good friends!)

We reached the door and the photographers, I composed a certain kind of face, developed a certain kind of self—a face and a self that I watched as if from the outside.

I was a married man. I'd broken my duck.

'Oooh!' sighed the waiting women. 'Aaah!' And the sun shone on us, exposing our shadows, the ulterior motive, the mental reservation.

My bride looked up at me, smiled, her smile said isn't it charming that they should think I'm beautiful; isn't it charming of me that I should think it's charming.

And I smiled down at her, wondered (for some reason) if they realised she had hair—hair, I mean, besides the profusion on her head.

We could still hear the tread of the organ's *ostinato*.

Cameras clicked, she looked at the cameras as if they were the funniest things she'd ever seen in her life.

I've since torn up all the photographs, but I still see her beauty on that day—a beauty that was not beauty, because not good. And that which is not good, is not delicious to a well-governed and wise appetite.

Dear God, the misery we concluded in that smart church between the Wagner and the Mendelssohn! There should be

76

a government warning. What had I done? I should've asked myself what I'd done, but you don't, not amidst the champagne and chandeliers of the South Kensington Hotel. After the detritus of slums, the blisters and mildew, I enjoyed the taste of all that pinchbeck and argentine. For her. And me. Reflected in every mirror. Gown by Hartnell. Morning coat by Moss Bros. Food by the ton. Chatter by the hour.

Waiters, courteous and contained, proffered knick-knacks, filled up the brittle glasses with a lot of yes-sir and no-sir, which would doubtless go on the bill.

The father of the bride couldn't resist a few words. His daughter, he said (or at least implied) had had countless offers from men of substance and standing, but had rejected them all in favour of an aging and impoverished nobody. One of those slum landlords from North Kensington—who, contrary to popular prejudice made no money out of tenants, and had, indeed, invited them to his wedding. (Though not to the reception, one noticed.) Such was the man, ladies and gentlemen, who had won his daughter's heart. The ladies and gentlemen, as you could tell from their murmurs, were not so discourteous as to remain unmoved.

But they mustn't think the girl was a fool, he wouldn't like them to think his own daughter was a fool, so he immediately added a hint or two that my poverty wasn't *real* poverty, it was an endearing kind of foible such as only the rich can indulge.

Smiling proudly, he kissed his daughter on both cheeks. I sincerely believe that he loved her more than anything else in the world, except the sound of his own voice.

Replying to his toast I thanked him for his kind words, and expressed great pleasure in having acquired such a capital father-in-law.

'Don't rely on the capital,' he interjected.

Loud laughter.

I recalled how he had once telephoned me at my house in North Kensington, catching me, if I remembered rightly, knee-high amid the alien corn. (Polite laughter.) ' "Come and have lunch with me," he said. "Today?" I said. "Yes," he said. I looked at the sundial. (Titters.) "All right." Only then did I realise he was ringing from Dundee.'

He slapped me on the back. The joke appealed to him. Was meant to. Implied there was money. He respected money—gave it symmetry and centrality.

A great man. Full of final judgements—reporting in direct speech what he'd said to someone, and what someone had said in reply, and what he'd said in settlement of the matter.

I moved among the guests, they'd been longing to meet me, knew I had a property in North Kensington, but what did I actually *do*? Everyone else in the room seemed to *do* something, even if it was only archaeological digging.

My kind of digging didn't count.

'What do you actually *do*?'

'He has interests in banking, insurance and oil,' said my bride, answering on my behalf, under the impression that it saved time. It's true I had a few shares in Cornhill, BP, and the National Westminster. (She omitted all mention of my farming interests, which were among the largest in North Kensington.) 'But basically he's in property.'

'Well, you should've had no difficulty in finding some-where to live.'

'Actually I'm moving in on him.'

'And his place is large enough?'

'Suitable for a couple with about forty-five children.'

'Oh, how very grand! I didn't realise he had a stately home.'

She shrugged. 'It's a home. But, between you and me, rather a monstrosity.'

'Victorian?'

'Grandiose slum.'

'In . . . North Kensington, isn't it?'

They spoke of North Kensington as if it were the North Pole, or the North Star—the north end of nowhere.

People at the top, and beyond help. Women with curls that spelt effort. Real estate men—I mean *real* real estate men, not like me.

They were wondering whether the marriage was built on firm foundations.

Ripe plum she's chosen.

Certainly ripe. Not sure about the plum.

I went over to a huddle of my relatives, autumn crocuses, introduced them to the bride. They didn't like her, I'm glad to say. It's important that your relatives should dislike your wife, then they'll be on your side when it comes to the divorce.

Everyone else thought she was divine, and couldn't understand why she should throw herself away on anyone so peculiar. (They were to know all along that I might murder her.) I'm not implying they weren't nice to me, but they congratulated me with a warmth that only astonishment could've generated.

'You've done *terribly* well,' said these antedaters of misery.

'Thank you,' I replied, slightly grateful. And I returned their smiles; but what I really saw was the eyebrows, the raised eyebrows, I was in a room of hovering birds.

Where did you say you lived? In North Kensington. Oh. *Is* there a North Kensington? We know *South* Kensington. So . . . presumably there must be a North. Yes, they remembered now, you pass it on the way to Newmarket.

Those who knew anything about North Kensington always spoke of it in terms that were somehow negative. If, on the other hand, I'd lived in the East End, they would've found that quite delightful; have asked me if I had anything to do with the Eton Mission, or Oxford House. They *did* admire

79

the people who worked at the Eton Mission or Oxford House. One invited them to one's table, because they looked after the poor of Stepney and Stoke Newington, who, as you know, had borne the brunt of the blitz: dockers and warehousemen; the deserving poor; they deserved all the help one could give them. But as for the people of North Kensington, *who* exactly *are* they? One doesn't seem to *hear* of them. What do they *do*? They're neither dockers nor warehousemen, they weren't even *bombed*. They aren't *anything*, really. They're the part of Kensington that isn't South.

'It happens to be my home,' I said.

'Well, you've married a very plucky girl.'

They all wished us the most marvellous honeymoon. But it seemed they couldn't hold out much hope for what happened after.

Then they turned to my father-in-law, told him he hadn't lost a daughter but gained a son. It was appropriate that they should address him in the language of profit and loss.

She was by my side, in her going-away dress, how lovely she looked, it both expressed the figure and fell in pure folds. How proud I was to be seen with her! How desperately I wanted to have her to myself. I wanted to pick her up and flash her at them; then hide her from them, keep her warm and dark, like the inside of a 'cello.

Her gloved hand leant across me and wound down the window. 'Goodbye,' she waved. And an applause of confetti fluttered amidst the porticos of calm South Kensington. Lots of good lucks, it was all perfectly heavenly, they'd enjoyed every wonderful moment of it. And now they were tying *Just married* to the bumper, because that's *always* fun. *Just married. No hand signals.*

The beauty of her! I couldn't imagine her ever being old. She was the winged woman on the front of the Rolls-Royce. And in twenty years' time, when I'd turned as hard and yellow as a quince, she would still (I was sure) seem the latest model.

I looked at her breasts, she noticed, smiled—smiled as if her breasts felt lovely to her, and lovelier for being looked at. I told her I loved her. She nodded; placed herself inside me; taught me life in a new rhythm. And the motorway sucked us along, the fields rotated past. 'I know,' she said. This was to be an always-love, without tomorrow or yesterday. And my thoughts twined about her, budded, put out broad leaves.

The permanent is nice, while it lasts.

We were on our honeymoon. We'd reached a place called Away—where the sun always acts as it should, the mackerel clouds drifted in one piece, we watched them from the balcony, our bedroom had a cast-iron balcony.

Choked with wisteria.

Then night. And stars fastened shade on the darkness.

'You're beautiful,' I murmured.

'It's dark, you can't see me, but thanks all the same.'

She was always so modest about her looks, you'd think they were of her own making.

'The dark is light enough,' I said.

She began undressing on the balcony, even though people were below.

'You can be seen,' I said.

Her hair was about her, her eyes kissed mine. 'Do I spoil the view?'

'Dotingly! As if it were your only child.'

She laughed. 'This is our first married night. Don't you think perhaps people ought to know about it?'

'They'll *never* know about it.'

She embraced me; prospected my back, let her fingers do the walking. Was I some Grampion? What did she expect to find?

81

I didn't ask her. Words barely came to us. In the darkness of love we reached the primordial silence that underlies all language. And there, *there*, I began to sense the magic of familiarity, the intensity of getting used to her—getting to know that body, feel it by heart, with the dark ME inside her. Such falling into place—as if we'd loved together all our lives; and I was excited as if we'd never touched before. 'I'd like to change persons with you,' I said, 'so that you can feel your own loveliness.' In feeling her I feel myself, my own nerves, not hers, I feel them feeling her, I feel her in order to feel myself. But I don't stay in myself, it's the *us* I want to feel, I imagine I'm the other half of us, I'm *her*, I'm touching *me*. Then I come back to myself, and imagine I'm a woman, she's a man. She's a colossus, oceanic, and I'm a tiny artefact she's given birth to. I imagine I'm her, imagining she's a man. I imagine she imagines she's me, imagining myself to be the woman.

What did it mean, all this let's-get-closer? This I-thee, me-her. Looking back, I wonder if it wasn't really a way of preserving the distinction between me and not-me, a keeping-the-distance-from. *I am you*, bring in the *am* to keep *me* from *her*. I think, therefore she's *out there*, the thing thought about.

We made love all night, the never-enough, having one's cake and eating it, then having it again; till, stupid with pleasure, I feel asleep.

But she awakened me with her hand—hand; lips; and her innumerable hair. 'I so want you,' she breathed. She'd discovered that a full vagina feels better than an empty one.

I didn't answer.

'Don't you want me?' she insisted.

'Yes, I want to, but . . .'

'But what?'

'I . . . can't. Any more. I'd like to, but I can't.'

She pouted, tutted. 'My Nanny used to say there's no such word as can't.'

And she coaxed my penis into a new erection, she liked that little bit of development, it was something of her own making.

Once again I was under the strength of her skin, her light shone in my eyes, the moon told me of day. Dawn too was of her own making, she seemed to call forth the sound of birds and rivulets. And the air was clean enough for lichen.

I was at the window, following the flutter of a butterfly's wings, its half-drunk tottering in the summer rankness, the so-accidental reaching of a flower, you'd swear the flower reached *it*. And presently I began dreaming of a pagan love amid thick-quilted meadows.

We wandered as far as the woods, made love in them, I loved their ancient freshness. A Londoner, my orgins were deep in the country: London was once deep in the country.

I taught her the business of the mouth, the chiasmus of *soixante-neuf*; and we gazed at each other as if nakedness were of our invention.

We met a cow in calf; watched the head-tilting of the great blue heron—till it flew into the distant hills, as if their blueness made them sky. We saw cottages; and houses: houses that grew from the ground, and cottages that had gone to bed in it. And neither knew any Local Authority, except the authority of local stone.

Thus we let the day invent itself, mind became earth, we invested it with grammar.

Yet my bride drew no enduring nourishment from nature. She became disturbed to see fields of sheep when they could more profitably be filled with blocks of flats. And trees had little meaning for her, because money didn't grow on them. In a word, she flagged when away from the k'dunk of Kensington; was homesick for the dust. Because she loved modern life, or at least lived it, lived life as life is. Whereas I, born at the wrong time, and in the wrong place, instinctively stood back from it, from all its indefatigable traffic—sometimes to admire, more frequently suspicious, and always a very Zulu of incomprehension.

Clouds, whereby God signifies His holy presence, find in me a worshipper.

Next morning we had rain, she always spoke of rain as if it were something to be endured.

'The forecast said fine,' she protested.

'It *is* fine. Fine rain.'

'I can get that in London.'

And back we went. A queue of cars from the Robin Hood Roundabout.

Some people hate rain; some don't mind it.

I love it. I mind every note of it, as if it were my child.

'No *sun*,' she said.

What nonsense! Of course there was a sun.

She never shared my unimportant pleasures.

CHAPTER VIII

And yet I felt so happy. She was a step towards a child. For this I was in love with her, was prepared to settle down and live solvently.

She fried me a fricandeau, imagine, last year I hadn't known her; twenty years ago she was scarcely conceived! And my house was already being transformed.

By the frying of a fricandeau.

We must have proper lavatories, she was a determined enemy of shit.

I introduced her to my charwoman, who wasn't my charwoman any longer, except that she was, I'd given her the sack, but she refused to go. She was soon to go of her own accord. Charwomen, it seems, prefer working for men. Not that my wife ill-treated her; on the contrary, she asked after the church, gave her an old dress, was upper-class kind.

Poor charwoman! She no longer called me *dear* and *sir* alternately. She no longer called me anything at all. 'Things aren't the same,' she said. She doubtless felt she'd have to do a stroke of work.

And me too. Not just hoeing the garden. My wife didn't like that. She knew I was the soil I hoed. So too in a distant way was she, and she preferred not to be reminded of the connection. 'You must *do* something,' she said. And she meant business.

She was terribly good to me; and *for* me; made me feel

I'd all my life been looking up a well. With a plait of her hair she was drawing me upward and lightward, my eyes were opened, I saw the nap through the carpet, the wood-pocks on the door, the weal in the linoleum. I factitiously believed in her, loved her, even if unconvincingly, and with a perfect fury of accumulated dishonesty.

She rang the builder, and along came three workers-of-the-world-unite, rain was seeping through the old York, a mushroom tenanted the basement ceiling. Their answer was asphalt. They called it ash-felt.

'Anything else need doing, madam?'

'Not now, or you'll get confused. And mind you don't leave any mess.'

'We'll clear it up for *you*.'

'It's part of the job.'

My tenants, extraordinarily enough, so far from appreciating her concern for the house they lived in, only wanted to be left in peace, as they called it. Poor derelicts! Perhaps they felt that her doing something for them would end in her doing nothing: that the house would become the sort where one didn't want derelicts to be.

I'm a bit of a derelict myself.

'If only you could put up shelves,' she sighed.

'Anyhow I have green fingers.'

But green was never her favourite colour.

Except the green of money.

'And get rid of the mushroom,' she said.

'The what?'

'Mush room.'

She made two words of it.

Would she renovate the whole house? She couldn't as long as the tenants were here.

Reading my thoughts she said: 'You'll have to give them notice.'

Oh, she couldn't defend it morally, she agreed about that; but unfortunately it was no longer possible to be moral on £5,000 a year. I asked her why she was so obsessed with money. After all, you can't eat it; it won't paper a room.

'You've mistaken the tense,' she said. 'Money is future. And at the moment we *have* no future.'

'Let's go to bed,' I said. Fucking is future, isn't it? At least a respite from irreconcilables. So, once again, we turned to that old club, the in-and-out of sex. I was now my penis, my brain was in its head. For a time there was no such thing as money. For a time there was no such thing as time.

'There!' said the Managing Director of Bethell, emerging from the bottom drawer of his desk and opening the *West London Mail*. Such was his air of triumph that I expected to see the report of a take-over, if not the establishment of some empire. 'Your wedding.' He wore tinted spectacles that darkened as the light brightened.

The photograph, it made me look like a murderer, and was to reappear in the national press at the time of the trial.

'And I hope you'll both be blissfully happy.'

'Touch wood,' said my wife.

But there was no wood to touch.

She (did I know?) perpetually astonished him: was so efficient that one forgot she was a woman; and yet if she wanted to she could be very feminine.

That, I told him, was part of the efficiency.

He remembered to ask about our honeymoon, though he was more interested in telling us about his own little trip. He'd been to Gambia, and Zambia. Buying and selling. Inevitably: because every situation is either a buying one or a selling one. Marriage. Even a holiday. You buy a Paris or an Istanbul. Paris is worth half an Istanbul. He showed us his films. Everything was screened. Screen and structured. You go through a door into a boardroom, you step from a plane into Gambia or Zambia. You eliminate what can't be bought or sold. You buy a tan; you sell an air of success.

You must always be booked up. The appointments you make must be months ahead. You must be in Gambia, or Zambia. It doesn't matter what you *do*, provided you're busy. The secret of success is to be always busy. Even if it's only lunch—business lunch. Or a holiday—business holiday. Make sure you never have time. Time is present. You must have only a future : projects. And a past : films. Yet your future is no future because choiceless; it's recorded in your diary like a past.

'Your wife,' he assured me, 'can achieve anything she sets her mind to. I've preceded her through a swing door, only to find she was on the other side before me.'

To change the subject entirely, he wanted to know if I would join the board. Seeing I had property. I protested that I was very small, but he said not to worry, they weren't after anyone large, they were small themselves, the large boys spoke quite a different language.

Yet he was interested in my remote connection with Wates.

Bethell were a midget by comparison. But at least they were a hundred per cent honest, he assured me. Though nobody's *that* perfect. Not that there was any evil in him; he wouldn't have killed a fly unless it were to his advantage. And yet I doubted whether (shall we say?) he'd be elected to the Athenaeum under Rule Two. He had upwards of a quarter-million, dispersed in various bank accounts at home and abroad, with a fine disregard for Her Majesty's Commissioners of Inland Revenue and the Exchange Control Act. With a formidable front in two junior ministers, he was in little danger of being had up for fraud, which is so difficult to distinguish from ordinary sharp practice. Abuses, it seems, are all right, provided you don't abuse them. Take tax, for instance: it was one of Bethell's maxims that tax was optional. And yet you must at all times maintain respect for authority. You might drive over the single line in the middle of the road; but not over the double line—at least, not very often; and you'd first look in the mirror to see the police weren't on your tail.

I was to attend monthly board meetings. Bored indeed, like some Baltic deputy, silent throughout; not that they seemed to mind, they even paid me, it had something to do with tax.

And my name appeared on the letter-head. (I wonder if they've troubled to remove it.)

These were to be my circle: men who never *see*, but have sight of; for whom there is no *now*—only moments in time; men for whom political wisdom was the evasion of tax, the bribery of local officials; whose magic number was neither three nor seven, but a million. A thousand thousand was nothing to a million. For them, I realised, Kensington was less a borough than a blueprint; and I found difficulty in remembering that houses were places where people lived. They forever talked about getting this or that building *off the ground*, which struck me as a most perverted ambition. They even talked about getting *roads* off the ground, and in this they've succeeded, as we know.

(I had never thought of it in this way) money was something you *made*. It was a game. You didn't work and get paid for it; you didn't inherit an estate that yielded x number of pounds; you planned, reconnoitred, chose your terrain, decided on your tactics. I rather enjoyed the idea: it reminded me of Oxford; or peace-time soldiering.

And all the while my wife sat in groomed loveliness, took notes of deals, and with a voice in proportion to her body, told them the growth of this, the yield on that. You would never have thought her smooth exterior could contain such engineering. There was a beauty about her manipulating; an arctic cleanliness in her point-making. And her shoulders seemed conscious at the tips.

I dreamt about my garden; and the soul of my unborn child.

Unconceived. He couldn't be conceived for some months, the whole board was unanimous, it had something to do with tax.

CHAPTER IX

Every night I made love with her; desperately—almost despairingly, such was my impatience. What's the point of marrying if you don't make children? If only I could've borne as well as conceived.

'I want him *now*,' I said. (Curious, he was always going to be *him*.)

'Then you'd better start making some money.'

And she turned her back on me, as if it were all over.

There were no curtains in the bedroom, but then I liked the faint rhombs that the streetlamps drew on the ceiling. I liked the way they revealed her body, while dissolving it into something incorporeal, so that the touch of her pale flesh was a shock of warmth. But she said people might see; for the honeymoon was over. The moon had waned, and soon the honey would sicken.

'You think a child's a toy,' she said. 'The type you wind up.'

'Oh, I know he runs on fuel, but, after all, we have three acres of vegetables, don't forget.'

'And meat? Does *that* also come from the garden? Hedgehog, I suppose. Baked in clay.'

(For her) gardening was a lost syntax. And the house seemed no longer mine. I was glad when she went to the office; glad to be alone.

Except for the calls. She would 'phone to ask me if anyone had 'phoned.

'No.'

'That's because you take the receiver off the hook.'

'Then how did you get through?'

She sighed. 'Do you miss me?'

'Yes.'

'Well, I won't know unless you tell me.'

'My body will tell you.'

And now, within weeks, after so many a fuck to no purpose, came the time for sowing, she conceived, the car started first time, it was part of her efficiency.

'I can feel him in my womb,' she said.

'Can you?'

'You don't sound very excited. Or don't you believe me?'

'Oh yes, I believe you. You're telling me what I already know.'

'How can you *know*?'

But somehow I did. I'd planted a man in her.

And I made love with her again. With *him*.

Is there sadness after intercourse? My child was condemned to a poor lifetime of sadness after that intercourse of ours. Myself, I was joy, joy, I was with him, I was *him*, in the darkness of the womb, forgetting we'd ever have to leave it. Again I made love with her, made love with her in front of the child, they say you shouldn't, but I was re-enacting his conception. Tiny body, appendage to a head, a single comma, I already wore your image, formed your face from old family photographs. After thirteen weeks you began to breathe, you were only four inches long. You could sigh, cough, hiccup. You could yawn. Yearn. Cry. Your mother drew in at a cigarette, and you drew in too, gasped for air.

My child! I loved you all your unborn days.

And now I could feel the beat of his heart, the kick of his

92

bone-curd, he could be born and live. My wife and I were now one, married in this child. We could separate, we could divorce, we could tear each other apart; but no man, except by death, could put us asunder.

'That gurgle,' she said.

Alarmed, I thought she meant the child. 'Gurgle?'

'In the bathroom,' she explained. Gurgle in the bathroom! And I, poor sot, so ready to feel romantic about her, to take her within the cunt of my arms.

'Does it really matter?' I said.

'There's no antispyhoning.'

'Oh.'

'And the outgoing pipe discharges into the valley-gutter.'

'Is that wrong?'

'It wouldn't really matter, except that the basin is where your tenants wash up.' (Always *your* tenants. A slight stress on *your*.) 'And I shan't like the smell when summer comes.'

She went up onto the roof (pregnant), I had to go too, me, with no head for heights, it's bad enough being six foot eight.

Leaf-clogged drainpipes; cracked slates; crumbling masonry: how did they view this hard-edged product of South Kensington? (They knew) she'd have the whole place down, and I not there.

She shook her head; seemed to be shaking her head at the whole of North Kensington. Then she turned, made me feel part of the dereliction. 'I thought all this was meant to be done.'

'It seems *I* was done.'

'And now it's past repair.'

(Or did she say *past prayer?*)

'Good,' I said.

'What?'

'I said *good.*'

No, she knew from my eyes, I didn't mean I'd applied for planning permission. No, dear God, let my ruin crumble on; crumble into oneness with the encroaching vegetation, till it seemed a natural growth, rising from, rather than settling into, decay. Its stone, which had managed so long without her, could've been coral, half formed by insects, half worn away by inundation. For me (you can laugh) it was a kind of Canaan, Ithaca, the final lap of an experiment. Not that it was what you (or I) would in fact call an old house, nor was it the heir to an older one. But built on fields; and nothing can be older than fields. Not that it ever saw them, for the surrounding streets were its contemporaries. Yet it had three acres of garden, which is a way of saying that something was left to itself. And it would go on being left if I had my way, especially as North Kensington, unlike the South, knew no other touch of green—not so much as the Georgian poetry of parks.

She stared at the rice in the valley-gutter, as if the secret of her destiny lay in those soggy grains.

'Tenants're vermin,' she said. 'Just as well the builder sloped off. As long as your tenants're here, you'll be chucking money down the drain.'

'How so?'

'Because they chuck *everything else* down it.'

'I could ask them not to.'

'Tenants're vermin,' she said; sighed at the surrounding streets : roofs covered by junk; a heap of dead stalks; men with black bundles, themselves black bundles; broken glass. The unpleasantness!—unpleasant in a wind because of dust, unpleasant in a calm because of smell.

Vibration—for we have none of those systems that keep heavy traffic at a distance from nice people.

Gothic ineptitudes. Or the shells of them. Against a

94

horizon of high-rise, boxes of boxes, the Lego of development.

I helped her down through the skylight, 'Careful,' I said, I didn't want my child to fall. I even helped her down the stairs, they'd never creaked so much, could my child make all that difference?

She released my hand. 'Just go up and come down again, will you?'

'What?'

'Do as I say.'

She stood underneath, I came down as softly as possible, but the staircase was laughing at me, splitting its sides.

'I don't like that,' she said.

'Never mind, it'll grow on you.'

'You make it sound like fungus.'

'Plants're part of desire.'

'You're too idle to make the money.'

'Oh, stop thinking about money.'

'Somebody has to.'

'You think of nothing else.'

(Must she remind me?) a child was on the way.

On the way? He was *here*. In a sense he'd been here all along, from the beginning of time, and before.

This was the ninth month, and the lordly purple placenta sensed the end of its task. Like most babies—this is their wisdom—he was born at night. Why wasn't I at the ringside? Doctors rather encourage it.

But I went to a dance-hall instead. The Palace. She brought that up in court.

I made for the drinks, couldn't bring myself to dance, then a girl came up to me in the ladies' excuse-me, an accountant at Cook's. Lived by herself in a bedsit, we weren't to make a noise on the stairs.

I said: '*Mutatis mutandis* I could fall in love with you.'
And she looked pleasantly confused.

'Time you were married,' she said.

'I *am* married.'

'I thought so. Doesn't your wife mind?'

'Being married to me?'

She was very patient. 'No, I mean . . . doesn't she mind . . .'

Oh, she minded! Yes, *and minded*. She was to mind and remind. The thing was, she'd telephoned, you see. She'd telephoned from the nursing home. Why didn't I answer, where had I been?

'I was at the Palace,' I said.

She frowned. 'The *Palace*?'

'Yes,' I said. 'It's the name of a dance-hall.'

'Oh. A dance-hall. Well, actually I didn't *think* you meant *Buckingham* Palace.'

She might've died, and what was I doing, I was fucking a *soubrette*.

'I'm sorry,' I said.

'Better if you'd *thought*, then you wouldn't *need* to be sorry.'

'I thought a lot.'

'You didn't think about *me*.'

But I did, I did, I was there in the womb, a different womb (I admit), but one womb is much like another.

'And I was getting a child,' she sobbed. '*Your* child. *You* were getting a child.'

But I *wasn't* getting him. I wasn't *getting* him, I already *had* him. And now, after nine months of living with him, I was to endure the torture of his birth. Not just the leaving of the dark and holy womb, but the thrust into those denting jaws, the tugging with that whole tower of instruments! And you expect me to sit at home. Puff a cigar. Drink. Masturbate, perhaps. No, fucking's cleaner.

'Is your wife at home?' asked the girl from Cook's, and me inside her.

'No. In a nursing home.'

'Is that her work?'

'Labour.'

Child! I'd take it upon myself, but the pain is yours, for all my regulated breathing, so carefully rehearsed. The pain is yours alone. Mine, too.

'It's a boy,' said the nurse, bringing him from a room marked 'No Admittance'.

'Of course,' I said.

She frowned. 'Well, they come in both varieties, you know.'

His face was one why. Why this suffering? What crime must he confess? What information did they want from him? They only had to tell him what he should tell them, and he'd tell them; then, perhaps, they would let him go back where he came from.

'Give him to me,' I said. And she saw I meant it, I held him in my arms, *in* them, could my love be a womb for him? 'Never mind,' I said. These were my first words to him, I was already speaking as fatuously as any parent to any child. 'It's pain usable,' I said. But he continued to cry, cry, we learn to cry before we laugh, first things first.

The hands of the clock met at twelve, feeding time, I passed him to his mother—who held him all wrong, 'You're holding him all wrong,' I said.

'Well, show me.'

God, she had to be shown—*Cup your arm!*—she was holding him like the dead Christ.

'He's beautiful,' she said.

'Not at all,' I said. 'He's ugly. Hair like a hearth brush.'

She brought that up in court too, but all I meant was that

D 97

you love your child, you love him, he doesn't have to be beautiful for you to love him.

He looked a million years old. Was. And all that time he had lain in me, he was part of my earth.

But his mother knew nothing of this, only the recapitulation in her own miniatureness, from which he emerged like some dwarf divinity, with untranslatable eyes, looking as if he could sway the whole round of existences. I watched him with sacred astonishment, I was afraid of my own baby.

Afraid *for* him.

The Thracians, when a child was born, wept. I could weep too, I saw him through a sea of unshed tears.

I heard the sister say to me: 'You weren't at the birth, were you?' And she took him away.

I'd only seen him for a few minutes, I feared I might never see him again, or only for visits, he'd been produced by The Authorities. And a Judge of the Family Division would arrange the hours of access.

Family division! In the womb he'd been so close, and now he was behind a door marked No Admittance.

'I have a child.'

I said it to assure myself. Even though he was behind a door marked No Admittance, I had a child. I would pass on the news to strangers in the street, they weren't strangers if I had a child.

I wanted to cuddle stray dogs.

A week of waiting. I counted the seconds like the twigs of trees, I counted the twigs of trees, each was preternaturally sharp against that whole sky of time.

A week!

You weren't at the birth, were you? Actually not. Oh?— where, then? Yer honours, I was fucking a *soubrette*.

And finally I murdered my child's mother, it all fits, right?

98

If I tell you I was at the birth in spirit, you'll make enquiries concerning the whereabouts of my body. If I tell you the nursing home wouldn't admit me, you'll check to prove me wrong. Wrong indeed, for it welcomes fathers. Oh yes, welcomes them—as long as all goes well. But as soon as our children really need us, our place is in the corridor; because our indifference can never be relied upon.

I saw it all. Kept seeing it for days. Nights, too. I would hear the plock-plocking of the Cardiff pump, plocking all the way down Kensington High. Poor foetal heart, you want to postpone being born, and so do I, but we must.

Then night comes, he knows it's night, and beautifully he comes spirally down, in the direction of his mother's hooked-up heels. You were only waiting for night.

Then you stop. Because a natureless light dawns on your dark sense : the white of wall, and overall, and a sun that hangs from the ceiling to ask you questions *or else*. Have you heard, child, of a deep transverse arrest? You were fine till you turned, did you do it deliberately, would you rather die than bow your way into that shadowless torture chamber?

There're no instruments, my child.

I say there're no instruments, don't you believe me?

I said it was dark but it's light. And with such a hurt of light, who needs instruments?

But instruments, too. A cuntful of needle, you'd think (wouldn't you?) this was all, but on top his mother screams, *don't scream*! Not in front of the child! When you're meant to be helping him. Breathe, woman, breathe, you've forgotten to breathe, breathe smooth and long, deep in, deep out.

It's a strange sight, knife cutting into cunt, and the midwife's banter. A gush of blood wraps itself round the lips of the anus.

Forceps, and my child's heart beats frantically fast, you could hear it in Cardiff.

Woman, get your arse down, the forceps can't do a thing if your arse is flying around, at best they only turn, they don't pull, *you must push*, push down, push long, into your arse and out.

And suddenly:

A head of hair crowning in that fork.

This was the known way, the way the head of Jesus, Son of God, crowned in the holy fork of Mary.

My child, your head has already crowned, the rest is child's play, but don't dawdle, you have five minutes to escape (No! Escape means *out*, you poor fool!)

Blood in your ears. Bleeding at the ears? Or maybe it's just part of the muck, you little dredged-up *objet*. Is the penis missing? So often the penis is missing. No, there it is, ready to repeat the whole volution.

Out of that gaping bloody ruin the cord hangs down, the scissors still sticking to the end.

Dark-age Goth, you're half-opening your eyes, as if to dispel the light that pricks them. You had only dreamt such cruelty, you now wake to find it true. The lids close, you seal them, screw them up, but the rays pierce, there's no escape, except back into the amniotic mud, and once you're out you're out.

You cry. Who wouldn't?

'Hello, *sir*!' says the bantering midwife. Poor archae-ological discovery, *hell* is the first syllable you hear: it's the old old word for light.

She turns on the tap, washes off the earth, my wife in origin is earth, I shall love her, she hoped I wouldn't know.

'This is your home,' I say. 'As you doubtless remember.'

100

He's so tiny, tiny. More complex than the sun. Lying un-appalled in calm and sinless peace.

I look after him through those first days and broken nights: clip and unclip the blankets in his cot; bring up his burps over my right shoulder; shake the talcum on his arse, tak-tak-tak.

He rests his head on my heart, comforted by its quiet pounding.

With love of him I feel faint, fortified.

I love his very shit.

I introduce him to the tenants; and to the plants. The plants suddenly grow. The tenants grow too, they even leave their rooms, their roots, to join us in the garden. I sing and they aren't embarrassed, neither the plants nor the tenants, there's a child, so they aren't embarrassed.

I sing to the spiky cactus till it feels no further need of spikes. I sing to the shallots, the boysenberries and the kohlrabi, who lean to embrace me, *me*, and I'm not Caruso.

I bless them, and they respond as only the blessed do, the very stars partake of their vibrations. Even my poor vermin will live to be alive.

Meantime my wife rested, but not idly, she read the Piagets and Spocks, they must've been simple in comparison with property specifications; yet she was careful to master every point, as if child-rearing were a £1,000,000 deal.

My child, you too had to learn, and there was no book to teach you, you had to work it all out by yourself from chance happenings, and your own experiments. What could you distinguish? You from not-you? Not even that. Only pleasure from pain. The one thing you knew was your mother's breast, and you didn't even know that. If you were removed from it you cried; but it wasn't the breast you were crying for, all you knew was the pleasure and the pain, not breast and not-breast.

Then you knew breast. I say *knew*; to be frank those fierce little head-shakes that made me laugh with joy were a search at random; but it was search with a purpose, and this is the genesis of all human endeavour.

I stand over his cot. He can't see me, but his eyes wander in the direction of my voice. I watch the movement of his hands; they touch, it's pure chance; but from this he learns, till chance becomes choice.

Later he'll choose to see me. And choose not to see me.

What he sees he can touch. Has he yet learnt that I can be touched when I'm not seen?

You know you have two hands, otherwise you wouldn't bring them together. You divide them; that's fun, because you know you can bring them together again.

Do you know your father from your mother? Probably not. You don't even know your hands from your feet, and stick both in your mouth.

I'm awed by your eyes' majesty. You are God. You've just made the world of things. You look at them. They're very good, but you wonder what to call them.

For the last half-hour you've been observing the shadows of thin leaves.

A building brick is resting on your blanket; not that you know the blanket is a blanket; or the building brick a building brick; the blanket could be an undulating plain, and the building brick a house; except that it couldn't because it isn't anything, you haven't yet reached the stage of things. That which I call a building brick, and which to you is sensation, feels your fingers; your mouth; it falls over the edge of your cot; disappears; and so does your interest in it. For it no longer exists. I pick it up, you look as if you've never seen it before. You haven't.

And to think that in ten years' time he'll be a boy like any other—all *bags* and *quis-ego*, and farts and feins.

102

Some of the vegetables had grown almost too heavy for my weaker tenants to hold. Poor vermin, I loved them like children; I loved them because I had a child. Especially my old gardener; who had time to watch the circling of twig and tendril and understand their feelings.

To make love with my wife was a form of gardening; I wanted to make love with her in the garden, for the garden's sake, but the house too was a garden.

'I love you,' I said. Felt her functions. Her tits were teats, she was a mother by the book. To be in her! In my child's birthplace! I hooked up her heels in my hands, 'I don't want to leave,' I said; 'you'll have to push me out, push down, push long.'

So she pushed; (laughing) pushed me out of bed into the cold room, where her hands were a tingling in the memory, my body's warmth was a sacredness which the air stood back from.

'And in ten years' time,' I said, 'he'll be playing the kind of cricket in which the highest scorer is Extras, making the kind of music that gives most pleasure to the performers, and putting *please* at the beginning of the sentence.'

She got up, stretched, a woman who without doubt did something for nudity. 'I'm glad you realise he won't be a toy for ever.'

'Imagine him in a cap!'

She avoided my smile. 'I can't imagine who's going to *pay* for the cap; and for the kind of school where they *wear* a cap.'

By a curious coincidence she was to make quite a habit of attacking me after love. 'Or am I to go back to Bethell, while you, a man, stay at home and mind the baby?'

'All right.'

She laughed. (I'd once so liked her laugh.) 'Do you think I enjoy being married to a lay-about?'

I was rather puzzled at her saying this, for she held 'without question' that child-care was ten times as tiring as any job.

'Why have you no *job*? Instead of spending the whole day on your lodgers and your garden.'

'That's as if you were to say I have no parents, only a father and a mother.'

'But parents aren't a *job*.'

(It's hopeless arguing with women.)

'I wouldn't mind so much if, for instance, you *wrote*. Then you could send the child to the local school, and everyone would believe you did it on principle.'

'No, they wouldn't, because you'd tell them I was plain poor.'

'But poverty doesn't matter if you write : it looks like dedication.'

'People don't write if they're happy. Give me something to mourn about.'

(I shouldn't have said that.)

And my child stared into the eyes of his marbles.

'Oh,' she waved, 'I'm not implying you have to be creative. Cultivate a speciality.'

'A cabbage patch. But I'm content with the cabbage patch I already have, thank you. I'm not interested in being the world's number-one authority on Lydgate.'

'Who's Lydgate?'

'Precisely !'

'Well, better than vegetating.'

I disagreed—having always been an admirer of the lilies of the field. And yet there was no denying that the postman delivered a whole tray of trouble. Every letter was an invoice, every invoice a final demand. The builders had stripped the walls, then left. Personally—though I couldn't tell my wife this—I relished the mottled plaster, patched with Carlite, like Pompeii in a cloud of paprika.

'Or Carthage,' she said.

'Carthage?'

'You could write about Carthage.'

'Hardly anything's known.'

'You're finding out.'

'I'll dig up the garden.'

'How will that help?'

'I may find something older and better.'

Suddenly she exclaimed: 'Those tenants. You'll have to get rid of them.'

'What?'

'Why do you *what*? You heard what I said.'

I was so tired of that asper tongue, the voice that was always several yards in front of her mouth.

'How in all decency can I get rid of them?'

'Decency is weakness,' she said.

And yet her beauty remained. *Such* beauty. Enough to start a stopped clock.

'Decency is weakness,' she said.

'I promised they would never have to go.'

'That was before you had a child.'

'What's the child got to do with it?'

'He's the real thing, so you can do without your substitutes, OK?'

'I love them more than ever.'

'Oh, do stop *playing*. Playing the lord.'

'I *am* a lord.'

'Lord of what?' she asked.

'A landlord.'

'You're a landlady.'

She didn't stop there. *I* stopped. Stopped my ears, in the hope of keeping the scenes from my child. Hope without hope. Not that he was any longer in the room, I made sure he wasn't, he wasn't even on the same storey; but scenes seep like rainwater.

No, not like rainwater. They will even poison my plants.

CHAPTER X

(Kissing his daughter on both cheeks) by Jove, he was delighted to see us! Shook my hand in both of his; asked us to pick what he used to call his brain.

I never felt at home there. I don't think my father-in-law did either. It was a place to receive in. Though genuine Elizabethan, it was maintained with such precision that you might pardonably have mistaken it for neo. 'Costs a fortune to run,' he said. But it ran like clockwork.

An estate agent's hour from Marble Arch.

It was rich in antiques; but somehow they seemed reluctant to make themselves felt: it wasn't the Hepplewhite love-seat you noticed, or the Chippendale screen, but the thickness of the carpet, the depth of the sofas, the profusion of plants, the shelves of unread classics, the litter of expensive junk. And when he asked me what I thought of his pictures I found I hadn't noticed them against the heavily embossed wallpaper.

'Elizabethan portraits,' he explained. Distinguishable from their Flemish contemporaries by the originality of incompetence. 'Bought them so long ago I can't remember what I paid for them; but I'm told they're worth a good deal, actually.'

'They're the sort of thing that'll soon be coming back into fashion.'

'Ah, I'm scarcely in a position to say,' he replied, rather as if I'd asked his opinion.

We had come early so as to taste the ordinary humble pleasures of the country, which so few can afford. Look out of the window and not a house can be seen. There's always great merit in not being able to see a house from your window.

'You must join the local hunt.'

To watch cats being chased round dustbins.

'We have two packs of hounds: one to hunt foxes, the other to keep the speculator at bay.'

We laughed. 'And the Local Authority? Who keeps *that* at bay?'

'*I* am the Local Authority.'

Again we laughed.

Others drove over from their country cottages. They had country cottages.

Second homes.

Second cars.

And other signs of debt.

Some (as I afterwards discovered) were broke. But broke on the grand scale.

A few of them farmed. It had something to do with tax.

A good party. All parties're good. Except that you aren't in a good part of the room. You look over the shoulder of the person who's talking to you, you plan your next move.

My wife passed round the farthing dip. 'You must be nice to them,' she whispered, knowing I'm normally quite ruthless about not meeting people I don't know.

'I'll be nice to them,' I promised.

And why not? They were nice enough to me. So I chatted from politeness with people I'd hitherto ignored on principle.

'If you're nice to them, they'll be nice back.'

Women with bosoms. Bared to dispel all doubt about it. And one or two dresses that were open down to *there*. Beautiful. Leisured. Beauty takes time. With hair piled on their heads, as if to make the most of so much air space. They possessed rich husbands, they'd chosen well. And chosen with some frequency, cutting out bridesmaids, love, and other inessentials.

But they adored their dogs.

'I have shih tzus.'

'Is it catching?'

'Oh, how *could* you! They're my little *toys*—toys disguised as powder puffs, and they go bow-bow. I have to wind them up every morning, and I put them back an hour for British Summer Time. Or is it forward?'

But their children they sent to Stowe.

Charterhouse.

Anywhere.

Their conversation was a joy. It had the fluency that marks those who can't think for themselves. They talked about the media. 'The medi*ar*.' 'The blame rests on the mediar—farly and squarly.'

They voiced the kind of liberal sentiments that often pass for thought.

By the way, how was it I lived in North Kensington?

(Had I blotted my copybook in the South?)

A-mazing. Ex-traordinary.

Their husbands were coarse-grained; friendly to a fault. So lucid. Shiny as looking-glasses. Without foresight or hindsight, vision or memory, continuity or conscience. So untouched. Except by tax. To hear them talk about tax, you'd think each of them was paying personally for Concorde.

'But money isn't everything,' said their wives.

Apparently not. I discovered in the course of the evening that there were also financial assets.

109

Diamonds.

It's the little things that count.

A lot of mental arithmetic: one of the wives had twins at Oxford (£3,000), and they still (touch wood) kept a cook and a housemaid (£4,000), but they might have to pawn the Rolls, ha-ha (£1,500), especially after their April in Alpbach (another £1,500). Total £10,000. Must be bringing in at least twice that. Pretty good.

We were twelve at dinner. When my father-in-law said twelve he meant twelve besides himself. I was thirteenth. I was thirteenth at every table. Not, mind you, that I'd have preferred to stay at home, my wife being so nice to me when her friends were around. She was even nice *about* me.

'I'm so glad you find him charming. He *can* be.'

And when they added how wonderful I was with the child, she so agreed; one must look on his positive side; one gets so tired of hearing unkind people call one's husband a wash-out. Why do they have to *tell* one?

Two MPs were discussing proximate questions; the good of the party. A tycoon, complete with ulcer, was talking about Gambia, and Zambia. Small talk. And big talk. The higher gossip. I was out of my depth. My wife had warned me I'd be out of my depth. Such *shallow* depth. Not a single murderer among them. No, no. Or even a married one. So boring. Which is difficult to forgive, though I suppose I should, because I bore a lot of people myself. At least there was my father-in-law. A giant. There were giants in those days, even ministers looked up to him. And yet he no longer really counted. Perhaps that was why they looked up to him. Respect (he knew) was suspect. He was a steam locomotive; exhibiting age's loss, age's gain, uncertain whether his place was on the tracks or in a museum. Familiar and withdrawn. An old master, people said. But was he even that? In repose he seemed unsure, and lacked the last-word stillness of great

110

art. Opposite sat his mother. Born under Queen Anne, she remained unmarred by any developments since the early 1770s. She would certainly never've asked me what I *did*. Whereas the women on either side of me, both very goochy-poochy, asked nothing else. I said I gardened, whereupon they replied how terribly *English* of me to tell them my *hobby*. Their husbands gardened too—it was the perfect relaxation after being stuck in an office.

'Yes,' I said.

There was much changing of the subject, I must've kept saying the wrong thing—till they became suddenly and intimately involved with their knives and forks.

You think I was rude. I was rude. Oh yes! Be not deceived: evil communications corrupt good manners.

My inadequacy as a conversationalist meant that our host succeeded for a time in commanding the table.

'. . . So I took a cab to Downing Street, braved the old lion in his den. And, my word, did he growl! "We (uh) gather" —remember his voice?—"we (uh) gather you want to (uh) go and *lecture the Americans*. Is this a time for gallivanting?" I protested that Gort and Halifax had done precisely that. "But Gort and Halifax," he roared, "*don't make guns*. Stick to your guns," he said, "stick to your guns." A pity. Otherwise (I sincerely believe) the Americans might've entered the war a year earlier.'

He didn't say on which side.

An impressive man; or at least an impressive figure—uttering his inconsequentialities with the sonorousness of a John Knox.

His mother leant across to me. 'Is that your daughter?' she asked. 'No,' I said; 'my wife.' 'Ah,' she said, 'I thought so: you look alike.'

She was the only one for whom I felt any tenderness; and when the Managing Director of Bethell, who was sitting

111

opposite, gave me a wink, I stared at it, as if he were suffering from some nervous twitch.

The women on either side of me made another attempt at conversation. They told me they lived in South Kensington, which was *so* convenient—meaning they could just *pop* into Harrods whenever they felt like it. Didn't—or were they mistaken?—didn't I live in . . . *North* Kensington? Really! How adventurous! I must've been the first person to go and live in North Kensington. A little *lonely*, didn't I find? Unless others follow. Perhaps they already have.

'Our child,' I said.

They laughed. They were delighted, I could make trivial conversation after all.

'Ah yes, you have a little . . . boy? Boy. An heir, you must be *so* pleased. Can he talk yet?'

'He says da, da, da.'

'That's hardly *talking*.'

Give alms; be compassionate; practise self-control.

I listened to these women talking, it was hardly talking.

My child! I was away from him. Out for the evening. His bedtime. He so enjoyed bedtime and a book, with me beside him to look through the pictures, you would think the whole run of the day was a preparation for this final pleasure. My child! Childhood's so short, a thousand or two of such bedtimes, that's all, and one of them has been taken from you, the world won't get it back.

To change the subject they wanted to know how the neighbours reacted to our presence, because the lower orders are so class-conscious, they don't seem to *want* a social mix. Whereas *we* tend to welcome it.

'More chance of finding a daily.'

They threw back their heads in a silent mime of laughter. And went on to suppose that North Kensington must be rather like the *colonies*, if I saw what they meant. With an

112

importation of natives to provide the right local colour.

'English,' I said.

'How do you mean?'

'The English are the natives.'

'Ah.'

Poor dears, they beautifully didn't understand.

'And what, may one ask, do these . . . natives . . . actually *do?*'

'Nothing much.'

'No big concerns?'

'Demolition.'

'But what about the little man?'

'Oh, there's the making of Molotov cocktails; and a few other cottage industries. But mostly they do nothing. The English're the last colony in the Empire, they're people to whom things are done: they're declared redundant, they're put on Social Security, they're evicted by the bailiffs when economics dictate. North Kensington isn't self-governing. It's a territory administered by the people in the South.'

'Rather nice of it to take the trouble.'

'Exploitation.'

'Really? From what you were saying, I gather North Kensington has very few resources to exploit.'

'Consequently,' said the Managing Director of Bethell, who was listening from the other side of the table, 'the South has let the North run down.'

The women on either side of me pursued the analogy of the underdeveloped world: we simply don't *need* their natural resources, let them *keep* them, we can survive on synthetics.

The Managing Director asked them how they would define synthetics.

Artificial.

But perhaps only the distinction was artificial. Plastics

derived from nature, and so did the mind that invented them.

There were signs of embarrassment. General topics are too intimate for a party. Get back to the personal, which reveals nothing.

The woman on my right asked me how my marriage was going.

'All right,' I said. 'And even if it weren't I would hardly tell you. I'd be asking you to dine with me at a table for two in the upstairs room at Rules.'

'What evening are you free?'

A pushing back of chairs, it was time for the ladies to retire, my father-in-law's mother leading, though she herself had to be led. 'Is that your daughter?' she enquired. 'No,' I answered; 'my wife.' 'Ah,' she said, 'I thought so : you look alike.'

The men sat down again, spread themselves cross-legged.

I found the Managing Director of Bethell next to me. He offered me one of his cigars.

'We got sidetracked,' he said. 'From North Kensington.'

'Ah. The colony.'

'Yes, you were absolutely right : exploitation doesn't cease to be exploitation just because the imperialist makes a loss. Indeed, the loss can be consequent upon the exploitation.'

'Then it's damned silly,' I said. 'No, thank you, I'm a non-smoker.'

'You don't cease to be a knave because you're a fool into the bargain.'

'Some bargain!'

'Oh, how right you are! Any objection if I . . .?'

I passed him the candle.

'Much obliged.'

'Not at all.'

'How right you are!' he repeated. Eye to eye. 'But you and I, if we put our minds to it, can make a much, much better bargain.'

'A unilateral declaration of independence?'

He shook his head. 'North Kensington must be peopled by the South. The South needs *lebensraum*, so let the North receive the overspill. Does that make sense?'

'And where's the money coming from?'

'Ah, that's the problem.'

But there was another problem: the prongs of his fork wouldn't go through the holes in the lace table-cloth, he was trying to get the prongs of his fork through the holes in the lace table-cloth, but the prongs were too close together, or, to put it another way, the holes were too far apart.

'The Council?' I suggested, trying to concentrate on the problem of *lebensraum*.

'The Council, it's perfectly true, will match us penny for penny up to twelve hundred pounds per unit of accommodation.'

'I see. Public money for private profit.'

'Oh, the Council don't lose: they put up the rates on the improved property. You follow?'

I was beginning to follow. 'And what about the natives? What happens to them?'

One prong, of course, can easily be inserted. So also, without much difficulty, can two: the first prong must occupy that side of the hole which is nearest to the second prong's hole. The third prong, however, falls slightly short, and the fourth very much so.

'The natives? They have everything to gain. A few lawyers and journalists around the place, and the Council will have to make North Kensington fit for lawyers and journalists to live in.'

'And what about the people who're evicted?'

115

He waved his cigar. 'Furnished tenants're extraordinarily transient, so it's misleading to talk of eviction.'

'Mine stay.'

Supposing one were to lift the cloth an inch or so above the table and insert the fork at an angle?

'It was yours, actually, I wished to ask you about.'

'You've been talking to my wife.'

'You could do for North Kensington what Buckingham Palace did for Belgravia.'

'I can't evict my tenants.'

'It would be morally wrong not to.'

CHAPTER XI

Not till much later did I realise—*really* realise—that *morally wrong not to* meant *there's something to be made out of this, and no one (by Christ!) will stop me.* Initially suspicious of that Managing Director, I soon became suspicious of myself. I should be *doing something.*

'You must,' said my wife, gently pushing the child from her; 'I mean, North Kensington's your baby.'

It was weeks before I answered.

'Bethell wants my tenants out.'

She crammed her hair into a Tam o' Shanter and complained of the cold. 'Just as well, if you ask *me.*'

(I *hadn't* asked her, as a matter of fact.)

'Just as well,' she repeated, 'from what I've seen of them.'

'Which is precious little.'

'If you *must* have down-and-outs . . .'

'They're very lonely people.'

'I'm not surprised.'

'Look, I refuse to stuff the house with white collar workers.'

'They don't have to be white collar workers. I wouldn't mind blue collar workers. But these don't wear any collars at all. They don't even work.'

I took the child's hand. 'That's *my* business.'

117

'Your *business*? Your business is with Bethell. Why were you so rude to the Managing Director?'

This, then was marriage: I'd planned it all my life. I hadn't planned it at all. Marriage!—where anything you say will be memorised, garbled, and used against you.

'I wasn't rude,' I said.

'You *were* rude. It went all round Kensington.'

'I'm sorry Kensington has nothing more important to discuss.'

'It *is* important. How often does anyone get an offer like that? They're prepared to bring you in.'

'You make me sound like a landed fish.'

'What *are* you, then? Landed gentry? Just *look* where we're landed! But the whole neighbourhood will move up if you do as Bethell suggest.'

'From lower class to middle class.'

'And why not? You make me so . . . Do you want people to live in slums for ever?'

'I want them to live where they belong.'

'Belong in slums?'

'What you don't realise is that everyone's different. Like locks.'

'*Not* all locks're different: every burglar knows that.'

All right, all right, but did she have to talk like this in front of the child?

'Do you have to talk like this in front of the child?'

Her mouth set in a thin crooked line. 'The child! What do you care about the child?'

'Look,' I said, 'it's a long time since we dined out, what about dining out, the break will do you good.'

'Dine out? You can scarcely pay for the child's pap. All you care about is your tenants, and you don't even care for *them*: you just enjoy playing Daddy. You neglect your child so that you can play Daddy to our candle-rent tenants.'

'Nobody'll be neglected if only we economise. For a start, there's no need to leave lights on, blazing all over the house.'

'Tell me,' she said, 'why do lights only blaze when they're left on?'

'I'm going in the garden.'

Maybe I said that to annoy her. The mere mention of garden was enough to annoy her. 'Garden!' she muttered. I couldn't *afford* a garden.

'You don't understand,' I said. Had she ever been known to plant anything in it? Only krugerrands. The situation, if I may sum it up, was that we had no money, and the Socialists were going to take it all away from us.

'You terrify me! Here we are, on the verge of bankruptcy—' Except that she said 'bank of vergeruptcy,' and I laughed, I hoped I might make her laugh too, I made the child laugh, I began singing an impromptu ditty about *the bank, the bank, the bonnie bonnie bank of ver-er-ergerup-tceee.*

Suddenly her nails grew longer. I was afraid she might poison my tenants; pull up all my plants. Why did she have to behave like this in front of the child, couldn't she let him laugh?

'You won't be able to treat him like a toy for ever,' she warned me. 'One day he'll grow up and have a mind of his own, and I can tell you what he'll think.'

'Or will you tell *him* what he'll think?'

'I could teach him to hate you, if that's what you mean.'

'Oh, I see, I see. You could teach him to hate me.'

'Easily!' she replied. 'Easily!'

'Good! I'm so glad! I mean, I wouldn't like you to be put to any difficulty.'

You infer from my reply that her words left me cold. Oh yes, they left me cold all right, they left me cold. Not—I must explain—that I believed she would actually teach the

119

child to hate me. No. But how, even in what was to become a war of nerves, could her mind frame this thought? And it was the thought of that thought which lingered on the extreme edge of my fear.

I bath the child, shampoo his hair, careful of the eyes, lift him with the towel around him; rub him through it. 'Dry between the toes.' I say this in my funny voice, he waits for it.

Take his vest and nappy from the radiator, feel them against my cheek.

How that child loved me! A child being so ready to love, I couldn't understand how any parent is hated.

He hates me.

He's been taught to.

We went into the garden, come on, quick sticks! I showed him the yellow broom, whereby Leopardi symbolised the precariousness of human life; and the cocksfoot grass for the cat to chew. The delicate veins of cabbage leaves; spring onions in an Arabesque, that won't stay still. I worried about the fallout of soot, and lead from lorries. Will the plants be poisoned? Will they poison? I teach my child how one leaf has a different character from another; teach him in the way an old athlete teaches a young one. 'Touch,' I say. 'Relax. Feel the give and take.' He removes his hands, which ripple and tingle, and the plants begin to sway. All Africa is within him.

Time for tea.

I pick him up in my arms, he makes himself part of me, sucks his thumb, a typical only child, more infantile than most, and more adult.

It's his dinner, he doesn't want any. 'Eat up! Mummy only says things once,' he says, having already said it three times.

He pats his food. Why do small children always pat their food?

120

'Please,' she says. Then *Please*! Till it graduates into POLICE! 'What're you *thinking* of?'

And his eyes reply: *What am I thinking of? I can only tell you my thoughts in a language that God would deign to speak; but you wouldn't understand; and into journalese it won't go.*

'Eat up,' I say.

I look at him in a trance of affection, doting on him. I dote in extremity. Love the toys of bulky wood, shaped by his touch. I'll never say of him as the Arians say, *Erat quando non erat*, there was a time when Christ was not.

I love thy very shit.

He likes banging old tins—the maximum noise with the minimum of effort. I buy him a hammer, and suddenly everything needs hammering.

His mother tuts. '*I'd rather you didn't*' becomes '*You'd better not.*'

'Somebody's going to get a smack bottom.'

He's a boy, in love with his mother, jealous of his father. He's a girl, in love with his father, jealous of his mother. This girl is jealous of me because I'm her mother, and she's in love with my wife because she's her father.

It's bedtime. Every evening he returns to the womb.

Tonight he wets his bed. First it's warm; then it gets cold.

His mother is angry in the morning.

'Never mind,' I say. Take him for a ride on the handlebars, his hair tickling my eyes.

I take him to Kensington Gardens—a London embraced by nature, and penetrated by it. Like the ancient Greeks, he's no admirer of views; but he senses the numen of the grove, and the spirits that haunt woods. I tell him the oaks are ancient enough to have been planted by monks, I ask him if he can hear the music in the heart of the atom, and I analyse the craftsmanship of the clouds. None of which he can under-

121

stand; and therefore is not bored. He enjoys the guardsmen in their red tunics, and the massed bands of geraniums. I watch his movements; the semantic use of the body. He returns to me; sits beneath my looks, with an inner tremble of eagerness, an unaverred yet prodigal inward joy. And his sympathy is no putting-on of words, but a naked physical outgoing. He seizes my cheeks, his teeth clench for love, as if he could murder me. I know how he feels: I've myself come at him like a murderer, holding him at rigid arms' length. There! Behold, this is my work and my glory. And the next moment I've grasped him to my chest, absorbed in him, absorbing him into me.

He's like one of those little rubber faces on sale before the war, he could be squeezed into any shape.

We ran around, perfect in joy, let the trot of the wind trample over us.

Then he rests against me. 'Even metals get tired,' I say.

And grains of grit have souls.

A gust. He's amazed how the trees only have to shake their leaves to make a gust that turns grass into sea. Not that he knows sea to be sea, he hasn't even been to the Round Pond, but there it is, he watches the little waves land up on earth, then return home.

On the bank are ducks. All kinds. By the dozen. He runs to say hello. But they swim away, he follows, learns a pond is made of water, that water is wet, and he's no duck. The verge slopes, he slips, and I run after him, slip too, we're both wet to the skin of our necks. This he considers the best joke in the world, and believes I invented it.

CHAPTER XII

Did I say she was a mother by the book? She was. Book knows best. I'd always been a bit sceptical of paediatricians, if that's what they're called, but when she voiced their theories I found doubt an effort. You think I'm feeble; after all, child-care wasn't property-management, it was a subject in which she was a child herself. But she had the knack of infallibility. Her very passing of the time of day was *ex cathedra*. Pope Joan! She would make a scene over some scene I was supposed to have made; it was never a scene, never more than a suggestion, but she took suggestion as criticism. Dear God, save me from the saints. Give me sinners, give me hell, but spare me her Holiness. I'll marry a *soubrette*, a witch, I'll marry an embezzler, seller of state secrets, receiver of stolen goods, so long as she's fallible—so long as she can fall. It's a fallen woman I want, not this pontiff of acerbity. Will you believe me when I tell you she used to hit that child? Perhaps you won't. But you'll believe me if I say I let her. I, who'd never knelt to technology, and distrusted its mercy-seat, let her; in the name of Piaget and Spock, and because she could pronounce between them.

She hit him once a day, I try to think it was only once a day, but it was more. A child no higher than my knee. Whatever harm he did, he'd paid for it in advance, he'd been born, hadn't he? But she hit him—I could hear it across the house—till I feared his bowels might burst through the skin, like a cat that's run over. (Even today) any sudden noise, a crack of thunder or the slam of a cell door, will go through me like jagged glass; and when I see a little child (which is mercifully almost never) I wince at his littleness.

But at the time I did nothing, just hoped that each smack was the last. Then: 'Kiss me!' he sobbed, running after her when he could hardly walk. 'Kiss me!' His despair! This was no mortal pain, it was hell, everlasting, no one had told him of death. The I-can't-go-on! He couldn't breathe for gasping. And yet 'Kiss me!' Strange. But stranger that I did nothing. I need a stranger word than strange.

Something burst in my belly; moved with slow pain along the shaft of my penis, as if to explode at its tip. Yet I took comfort from the sheer unbearableness of his convulsive sobs, she could never do it again, not after that, she could never do it again.

She was screaming at him, how could she *scream* at him? But at least she wouldn't hit him, not this time; this time she wouldn't hit him, she was screaming at him instead of hitting him, you don't scream *and* hit.

But she did; in accordance with Piaget (or was it Spock?) who said you must explain why you're punishing before you punish.

I went to the Welfare Officer, 'Were there any witnesses?' she enquired.

Unfortunately my wife had omitted to call in the vicar. 'Not besides myself,' I said.

'You aren't the witness; you're the plaintiff.'

'Oh, I haven't come here to complain. I want your advice, that's all.'

'You wish for my advice as to how you should proceed with your complaint.'

'I'm concerned with welfare; my child's welfare. Have I perhaps come to the wrong department?'

'Does his body bear the marks of beating?'

'His eyes,' I said.

She was on the side of the woman, and I was beginning to learn that I was alone, which did me good, I now knew how my child felt when his mother beat him and beat him, and his father sat in the next room; and sat. In the next room.

The prison shrink insists I was scared stiff of her. I don't think I was scared. But there was something about her that reassured me. It must be right to hit a child like that. I really thought so. Though few of you will believe me. But few of you have ever known my wife. And I don't know how to persuade you of the truth; or even to describe it. It's as if the Earth, suddenly awakening to the existence of machines, should deduce from their intelligence, and even from their beauty, that they would never do it harm; and therefore never rose against them—not, at least, until its fauna was poisoned and its flora starved.

Similarly I let her go on. And if I now tried to be around at his changing time, it was not because I doubted the pain was right for him, but because the pain was too much for *me*. Sometimes I'd be answering the door, or the 'phone, when his mother approached him. It's surprising how often she approached him when I was answering the door, or the 'phone. Then my child would run to me, because he knew I'd change him without hitting him, he knew he could be changed without being hit.

'Why don't you hit him?' she said. 'You're afraid to. I always knew you were a coward.'

So finally one day I hit him. I thought she could be right, I ought to hit him too, he'd be perplexed if he was hit by one parent and not the other.

How then he cried! Inconsolably, more than if he'd been hit by his mother. Not that I'd hit him hard. I don't think I could really have hurt him. He was inconsolable that I'd hit him at all. Wasn't I the one who didn't hit? What hope had he now?

I knelt and embraced him, 'My child!' I said, 'I'll never hit you again, never.' His mother was still there, but it was as if she weren't. 'Don't cry,' I said. But he went on crying because tears are a form of tenderness, they were his response to my own sorrow. 'I'll never *never* hit you again,' I said. But I knew this wasn't enough : I must see he wasn't hit at all.

Except that I couldn't : I couldn't be there always. So next afternoon, at changing time, I kept out of the nursery, waiting. I heard her say to him: 'Come *here*!' 'Daddy!' he called. I opened the door, he was coming to me; she screamed at him. You scream before you hit, in accordance with Piaget. Or was it Spock? Anyhow, she beat by the book.

Her back was bent, her knees gripped his tiny torso.

'Do you intend to hit him?' I enquired.

She looked up, as if my voice—it was peculiarly calm— were a thing visible. 'Somebody has to,' she said. 'And as you're only interested in the fondling and the fooling, because to you he's no more than a toy, that "somebody" has to be me.'

'Please don't hit him,' I said. 'He thinks the nappy's for shitting in. Who's to say he's wrong?'

In her eyes was complacency of evil, it had taken up the freehold. 'You coward!'

'All right,' I shrugged. 'I'm a coward.'

'You mean it's *not* all right.'

'Maybe I do.'

'Well, who's going to hit him? You or me?'

'Listen,' I said. 'Give him a rest. He's known the pangs of childbirth, isn't that enough? The pangs of a child at

126

birth. Have you never imagined what *that* must be like?'

I thought for a moment it was me she was going to hit. 'And when have you imagined *my* pangs? Giving birth, and knowing my husband was fucking a *soubrette*. That's what my pangs mean to you; that's what your child means to you : a chance to fuck a *soubrette*.'

'Therefore you're punishing the child.'

'Am I to ask *your* advice?'

'Don't hit him,' I said. There was menace in my no-menace.

'Get out! Stop fussing around the nursery and do a day's work. *Man's* work. Next time I'll marry a *man*. There's no room for you here, the child doesn't need two mothers.'

'He doesn't need two like *you*.'

'I see. You (you don't have to tell me) you'd be glad to see me dead. Wouldn't you?'

'No,' I said; 'I just wish you'd never been born.'

'I knew you were a coward.'

'Perhaps I am; the type who allows himself to be provoked by women; and physically assaults them; almost as bad as women who attack tiny children.'

'Your decency!'

'Decency is weakness,' I said.

Her eyes dilated. 'Don't you dare!'

'Dare?'

The child was crying desperately, I too felt desperate; yet somehow cool at the same time, for this was an emergency, I'm quite cool in an emergency, which may surprise you, you've doubtless decided I'm neurotic, but it's typical of neurotics to be cool in an emergency. The same when I murdered her. WIFE MURDERED IN COLD BLOOD. For once the headlines were true.

Of course, I should've murdered her now, not waited all those years, till the damage was done.

But at least I gave her a beating. I gripped her by the ears, wasn't it by the ears that I'd first caressed her? She didn't waste time by screaming, I admire her for that, her nails were straight at my eyes. But I downed her by those ears, her head was at my waist, she'd have bitten my genitals if I hadn't brought my knee into her groin.

Then I raised her face to mine, our lips were almost touching.

'In front of the child!' she sobbed.

'Yes!' I said. 'Yes!' And with her neck in my left hand (she thought I was going to throttle her) I thrust her head between my knees, she was powerless, nut-crackered.

Do you like the sound of ripping? I love it: it reminds me of that moment when I tore the clothes from her. My child, mothers have bums too, and their bums can be hit.

By God they can!

And then I saw my child's face.

'My child! I'm doing this for *you*, turning the tables, there's no need to cringe, it's your mother's cue to cringe, so feel free, skip, sing, shit in your pants, shit on the floor, shit all over the garden, and she won't dare so much as touch you.'

He was still sobbing. 'Come!' I said. But he shrank from me, it was the first time he'd ever shrunk from me, why should he be afraid?

The heaves of his body! The heaves seemed bigger than the body, he was all fear, the fear was frightening. The prison shrink says I was afraid of my wife, but I was afraid of my child—not afraid with wonder, not now, but afraid with fear.

For he would never recover. When the sea's a storm, can you imagine calm?

My hand he avoided, my arms he pulled away from. 'You're my all,' I said; 'I'll never harm my all.' And I *meant* all. As for my wife, as for *her*, she at that moment existed

128

not. I was my child; and on happening to notice the female body in the corner, as huddled as when she undressed for me on that first night, only now did I hear her tears. 'Go,' I said, 'get some clothes on, or whatever. And shut the door behind you.' She did.

I turned again to my child. 'Mummy!' he sobbed.

'My child, keep your shit and forget about lavatories, you know it's nothing to waste. Why send it to pollute the sea when it can replenish the earth?'

Picking up her torn clothes, I threw them in the bin, amidst his nappies and the shit.

'Don't worry,' I said. 'Daddy's going to make sure she's all right.'

I felt a hypocrite. Almost apologised.

And once inside the bedroom, seeing her stretched there, a heave of sobs, so like my child's, I felt a sudden surge of care : she too was in pain, she was my child; I knew (though not when) that I'd given birth to her, and I touched her flesh as if it were still my own.

All sex is sin without this sense of blood-tie.

My hands came between the bedspread and her breasts, she didn't stop me, her breasts were her tenderness, her vulnerability, she wanted me to feel her breasts. The sobs continued, but the waves were subsiding to a swell, till the swell became love.

Next day the child developed a twitch. I spoke to him and he stuttered. I held him in my arms, he wouldn't twitch in my arms. But he did. And the stuttering grew worse, he gasped for words as if they were air, heaving upwards as if to the surface, eyes unfocused, the work of it! Then a whimper of despair : he couldn't reach.

'Can't you find the words?' I said. 'Let's look for them together. Up *there*, are they? So high as all that? Goodness,

E   129

you'll have to grow, I can't even reach them myself.'

He laughed. (I'd feared he might never laugh again.) Perhaps the laughter would bring back the words. But it didn't. It only brought back the twitch. And he cried. Because the words wouldn't come. And sometimes he just cried.

Cried for the slightest reason. Or none at all.

And twitched.

His mother was very patient with him.

I said: 'I can't forgive myself for not having stopped you before.'

'Stopped what?'

'Stopped you from hitting him. I should never've let you start.'

'You're blaming *me*, are you?'

'I'm blaming myself.'

'And about time! You assault me in front of the child, terrify him, he thinks you're going to murder me, you nearly did, I wish you had; and now that the child's a wreck you blame *me*.'

'So glad to see you've recovered your usual spirits,' I said.

'You beast!' she screamed.

Why had I hit her in front of the child, when I should've killed her behind his back? She would never change. She dare not hit him, but she could scream at me in front of him. I said: 'Please, don't scream in front of the child, you know it tortures me.'

'Trust you to think of yourself, you wouldn't think of *me*! Torture! How do you think *I* felt, giving birth to a child and knowing you were fucking a *soubrette*?'

'All right, I'm sorry.'

'You beast, you think it's enough to say sorry. *Sorry*, he says!'

Her hands searched for glass, china, anything that would smash, she smashed it on the floor, against the walls, even threw it at the ceiling. And I, in a mime of calm, bent down and picked up the pieces, the bigger of them, taking them to the kitchen and dropping them into the pedal-bin under the sink; then returned with brush and pan to sweep up the chips.

'I don't think I've left anything,' I said. 'Anyhow, the cleaner'll be here in the morning, she can give it the once-over, OK?'

'What you've done to my nerves!' she sobbed. 'I never used to be like this. Can't you just go? You've got your *soubrette*.'

'And the child,' I said pointedly. Though perhaps I should've apologised. Please forgive me for being shouted at.

She replied with calculated fury: 'We'd be better off without you.'

Suddenly I was weeping. 'God, I should've known from the start what you're like. Blessed Virgin Mary!'

'I hate you!'

'You're a disappointed woman. You found you couldn't conceive parthenogenetically.'

'I don't know what that means. And I don't want to. Just go. Join your *soubrette*, she'll be impressed with your silly long words.'

'You don't want a man.'

'No? A man is just what I *do* want.'

'And I for my part (let me confess) wouldn't mind a woman.'

'I know *your* idea of a woman.'

'Please!' I implored. 'What sort of home are we making for the child?'

'Find your *soubrette*.'

'I don't want a *soubrette*.'

'Then fuck yourself!'

131

Lord God, if only I could! If only I could've begotten, conceived, and borne!

Failing that, what must I do? I'll play along with Bethell, or there'll never be peace.

Give my tenants notice.

For my child's sake I would give notice to my children.

'And do it *now*,' she said. 'There's no point in letting the grass grow under your feet.'

At each door a current of pain ran through my abdomen.

'Good morning.'

'Nice one.'

'I'm afraid you'll have to find alternative accommodation.'

But where? Not from the Council, being unmarried; not from the private landlord, he'd take one look at them. It's the old story, and I won't bore you with it: when a commodity is in short supply, the poor suffer and the rich don't; the rich continue to alternate between their London flats and their country houses, while the poor go from pillar to post.

One, an out-of-work actor, disappeared within hours—leaving black milk, green bread, and the kind of smell that Alsatians are trained to recognise.

A Jamaican—'Christ is the Head of this House'—went back to Jamaica.

The rest applied to the Rent Tribunal.

Except for my old gardener, I hadn't yet told him. I *couldn't* tell him, could I? Poor old man! All forgetfulness and involuntary farts. Well, perhaps he'd be better off elsewhere. I tried to think of the water that oozed through the walls of his room. And the dirt: dirt under; dirt behind; dirt too high to reach. Dirt ingrained in distempered walls. Floors of haircord and dust—it was difficult to make out which was the haircord and which was the dust. The windows of war-rolled glass, neither plain nor frosted. Details such as the

132

broken sash cords, the uncurtained half-landings, doorknobs with an inch of play; rusted coat-hooks. Mange.

(I said to myself) all this might've been seen to, but they wouldn't have thanked me for it; an unscratched chair makes them apprehensive, the landlord'll say they've scratched it, so they scratch it, and then it's a scratched chair. Open the window to let the stink out, and they'll say the room's no longer theirs.

'I can't make an exception. It wouldn't be fair, you see.'

He raised his eyes to me, my face had never been such a long way up.

I said I was sorry.

He looked at me as if I was apologising for my height.

'You'll have to go, I'm afraid.'

'You promised me . . .'

He didn't trouble to finish the sentence.

'I'll find you somewhere else. Somewhere decent—a home for the disabled.'

He shook his head. '*This* is my home.'

'You'll have a better one.'

'I don't want a better one,' he said. He didn't *want* a bathroom of polished tiles. Or a bog that flushed first time.

'Why ever not?'

'I know my place,' he said, as if that explained everything.

'Ah,' I said. 'You know your place.'

He knew his place. Perhaps it was the same with all those people in the surrounding terraces, condemned by the Council because the white of their stucco had turned to bruise or dung. You can't let people live in bruise or dung, they wouldn't like living in bruise or dung. Except that they do. Because to them it's the colour of their houses, of all houses, it's the colour that houses are.

'I know my place,' he repeated. He knew his place. And in his eyes was reflected all that I'd tried to keep out of mine :

133

the dark oak panelling; the weighty newel that his hand had daily rested on; the corners that no light reached; the known number of steps, the recognised unevennesses; mouldings that collected dust, and served no purpose, except that he had learnt to love them; vegetables that tasted of vegetables, and of the fact that we'd grown them.

I wanted to cry, I hated him for making me want to cry, I wouldn't have minded if I could've cried, but I couldn't, couldn't, there're times when tears are unclean.

He cried; he had a right to. 'Do you remember how you stopped and gave me that lift? And how you carried me from the car like a child?'

'Listen,' I said, cutting him short. 'I sympathise with your position. And now I must ask you to try and sympathise with mine. The house, believe me, is in a deplorable condition. Even dangerous. That's something I hadn't realised until . . . But now I do. And I must see to the necessary repairs. You'll have to leave because no builder would agree to work round you. And things can't be left any longer. I'd be a poor landlord if I left them any longer. However costly they may be. And they *will* be costly. Costly in the extreme.'

He was silent; and quite calm—the tears had passed, his calm seemed to grow from the passing of those tears.

I added: 'Only an increase in rents will cover repairs of this magnitude.'

With the aid of his crutch he went over to the sink, filled the kettle and put it on the ring, waiting there till it boiled, as if to spare himself more steps than necessary; took a tea bag from the mantelshelf, put it in a cup and poured on the water. He didn't ask me whether I too wanted a cup. Rightly, I think. But sipped in sad absent-mindedness, as if quite alone.

Then put down the cup on the draining-board. The spoon tinkled in the saucer. 'You're doing the repairs to get the increased rents.'

134

'That's unkind,' I said. 'And untrue. I've never thought of making a profit.'

'Not till *she* came along.'

'She?'

'Her.'

'Listen,' I said. 'I quite understand how you feel, but my wife can't be blamed for a decision that's entirely mine.'

Although this decision, as I made clear, was final, I was prepared to discuss it with him, but he refused.

'I'm sorry you're so unreasonable,' I said.

My wife rang up the Managing Director of Bethell, she sounded happy, I was happy she was happy. She was the jewel for which I would throw away my whole tribe. 'I'm so happy,' she said. (What change!) she was even happy when waking, when woken by the child, who, having learnt to unfix one of the bars, could escape from his cot, even toddle to our bedroom, 'Good morning!' I said, 'gooood morning.' Up on the *ing*. His face was a thesaurus of joy, it couldn't have been more joyful if he'd laughed, he didn't laugh, the joke was nothing, all that mattered was that I felt like making it.

He still stuttered, though. And twitched.

CHAPTER XIII

The Rent Tribunal is very different from a court: no royal
coat-of-arms hangs in the bare room; the Chairman and his
two associates sit at a simple table, from which no dais
divides them; and no lawyers divide us from ourselves, consequently we can speak in person—not that rent cases are
any simpler than murders or divorces; it's merely that no one
has yet had time to invent a ritual of the required hierarchical
complexity.

'Do sit down,' said the Chairman. And his lips counted
we were all there. I remember how he leant forward, whereas
Judges lean back.

Addressing the principal tenant: 'How much rent do you
pay?'

'Three pound ten a week.'

'Do you mean three pounds ten, or three pounds fifty?'

'Three pound fifty.'

(Cupping his ear) 'Speak up; I'm only human.' And to
prove it he was wearing neither wig nor gown. 'I'm only
human. As you are.' And he wrote down: 'Three . . . fifty.'

'I used to pay two pound.'

'What?'

'I used to pay two pound.'

'I see.'

'That's in the old currency.'

The Chairman opened his folder. 'You've . . . received notice to quit and deliver up possession on the expiry of the next four weeks of the tenancy which will ensue after the date of receipt of the notice. Now, you realise the landlord has a right to his own property, so what have you done about finding alternative accommodation?'

No reply.

'Will you have gone by the time the notice expires?'

'Don't think so.'

'Why not?'

'We want to stay.'

'Have you brought your Rent Book with you?'

'Yes.'

'Hand it to me, will you?'

The Chairman put on his glasses, which moved down the columns of rent and arrears. 'Nothing for a month,' he said.

'Until the landlord mends his roof we're withholding our rent.'

'You realise that's illegal?'

'Not so illegal as a leaking roof. A leaking roof's a bloody crime.'

'No, a leaking roof, it so happens, is not a crime.'

It's only very small things that the law cares about.

'If that's not a crime, I'd like to know what is.'

The Chairman removed his glasses. 'You're suggesting that the landlord has failed to look after his property.'

'Bloody shambles.'

'Well, if it's so bad, why do you want to stay?'

'We can't find anywhere else.'

The Chairman turned to me. 'When do you expect to repair the roof?'

'As soon as I get the rent, sir.'

His eyelids, so tired of lies, temporarily sank, pulling his face down into his chest. 'I see. So your builder is ready to undertake repairs while the rooms are still occupied.'

'Yes, sir.'

'Then why did you give your tenants notice?'

'Well, if they stayed . . . some inconvenience might be caused.'

'To the builder or to the tenants?' he enquired. (Didn't he know men had wives?)

'Well, both, sir.'

'So you want the rooms vacant.'

'As soon as possible.'

'But as long as they're vacant you won't be getting any rent, will you?'

'No, sir.'

'Yet you'll still be able to afford the repairs.'

'Yes, sir.'

'I suggest you allowed the roof to go on leaking in the hope that it would force your tenants out. Is that it?'

'No, sir. It's just that there's no point in working round them if they'll shortly be gone.'

He turned to his colleagues, asking them if there was anything they wanted to say. No.

Again he leant forward to me. 'If you were in our shoes, how much security would you give them?'

I said : 'Twenty-eight days, sir.'

He put his hands on the arms of his chair, and drew in a deep breath, which apparently helped him to rise. 'Wait, will you, while we confer.'

For the next five minutes I was alone with my few tenants, and an awful lot of silence.

The number of seconds in five minutes is three hundred. More if you count them.

Then the door opened. Jesus Christ won't look the same when He returns as Judge, and the Chairman of the Kensington Rent Tribunal also returned with an air which was indefinably different.

'We give you twenty-eight days' security,' he declared, glancing along the line of tenants. 'At the end of that period you have the right to ask for further security, but we shall only grant it if you can show that your failure to find alternative accommodation is not due to any lack of diligence in looking for it.'

I hated my return home; hated being hated by tenants to whom I'd been a father. Nature himself was outraged, and my garden would never taste the same. But my child ran and met me as excitedly as ever, I'd feared he wouldn't, half-felt he shouldn't, but I hugged him longer than ever before. *He* must be my tenants.

My wife also came to the door, how did I get on?

'We were face to face,' I said. 'It was horrible. They spoke as if they hated me.'

'The Tribunal?'

'No, the tenants.'

'It doesn't matter about the tenants. What did the Tribunal say?'

'Twenty-eight days.'

She drew in a breath. 'I don't believe you!'

'No?'

'But that's unheard-of, they scarcely ever give less than six months.'

'All I know is they asked my advice on how much security they should give, and I said twenty-eight days.'

'But that's the minimum.'

'I know.'

'And that's what they were given?'

'Yes.'

'Truly?'

'I swear.'

139

'But you're a genius!'

'Yes, it's a funny feeling.'

And it was a funny feeling to be hugged by her, she was *triumph*, we'd be happy ever after.

'Your tenants must be furious.'

'They turned on me.'

'How *could* they?'

'Why shouldn't they?'

'Vermin!'

We even made love, it was nice.

And in the morning she 'phoned the Managing Director and told him about my success. Why didn't he get me to represent Bethell when their tenants applied to the Rent Tribunal?

Yes, he'd be only too happy.

Everyone was happy.

Even me. I was happy for my child, he'd never seen us happy together, he was happy at finding such happiness.

And I thenceforth sat in Rent Tribunals, I was so good at getting out tenants.

'What does your husband *do*?'

'He works for Bethell.'

'But we thought he was merely . . .'

'No, no, he actually does something.'

I got drawn in more and more. At first I couldn't tell a claim from a permit, or an option from a lease. I didn't even know that you never send rubber cheques *back*. But I could ask the Managing Director. He in turn asked my wife, playing Pepsi to her Cola, he didn't seem to mind.

I respected her. She took care never to be late, or ill-briefed, or to be seen in the same dress twice. Even when the office was full of people she had the awe-inspiring self-absorption of people who are alone and unobserved. More art

140

than nature; more object than being. The stillness of the machine; and the power. Not the great machines of the iron age of industrialism. But delicate; all-penetrating.

Bethell taught me how to deal with the troublesome tenant in a perfectly law-abiding way: to be sure, they went round with Alsatians. (To be *doubly* sure.) But they didn't *use* them. It's merely that the tenant's less inclined to *argue* with an Alsatian.

The twenty-eight days were up, and my own tenants hadn't left, so on the twenty-ninth I applied for a possession order. A wait of thirteen weeks for a hearing at the County Court, which gave them a further twenty-eight days. Another fourteen days till the bailiffs appeared. All rather Byzantine, but at least (at last) they were out. And the proceedings were at the taxpayer's expense, so it didn't really matter.

They were out! But their rooms seemed so empty—emptier for the smells they left; and they left very little else: old egg on the oilskin table-cloth; mould on the used tea bags; a pile of *Playboys*; and *German in Three Months without a Master*.

I hadn't asked where they were going. What did it matter? Exile is *from*.

'Thanks,' said my old gardener. He wasn't being sarcastic. I felt I had one leg.

CHAPTER XIV

Things were looking up for my battered baby : he was now a nervous child. The stutter was disappearing, only the twitch remained, thrusting his mouth into a grimace. Each time he did it I thought for an instant he was smiling.

There wasn't a great deal to smile about.

But he enjoyed exploring the rooms where my tenants had been. And this was ironical, for I now told myself his disturbance was my punishment for evicting them.

I seized him, he laughed, what struggle to escape! I embraced him longer, I was embracing my tenants.

Where *were* they? Their cache of darkness had gone with the gravy-coloured curtains, my wife opened the windows, their smell must go too, she'd have liked to fumigate our memory of their ever having been here.

My poor old gardener! Away from his old food, his old lodging, his lodging too was food, it was what made living taste like life. I should've stood my ground. Yet I'd had no alternative; suddenly there was a world shortage of alternatives. Because I couldn't afford a scene. And yet maybe she was right, the house was getting a bit wheezy in the windpipe, creaky at the joints, it was clutching its back, complaining about the weather, shaking its fist at passing lorries.

'Any idea how much it'll cost?' I said. 'To do it up.'

'The whole house? Oh, twenty or thirty.'

She was quite casual about it, but the words to me were a sudden sentence, a fine I could never pay.

'You mean . . . twenty or thirty *thousand?*'

'Maybe fifty. I'm no surveyor.'

'But we haven't the money.'

Her thumbnail sank into the wood below the basin. 'Of *course* we haven't the money. You must make it.'

'By evicting tenants?'

'Their rent didn't so much as pay for the water.'

Yet we'd survived, my tastes were simple, I was happy to sit in front of the fire and read some book I'd read before. All right, my tenants were dirty, most of them, and the rooms were a sad-awful sight, full of splurges, as if left outside in all weathers; except that no rain, not even North Kensington's, could have made it as dirty as that. You'd think God in His wrath had turned the world upside down, so that all the oils and effluents could splash off the clouds. Yet what harm did they do? It's cleansing that really dirties; detergents pollute, and there were a lot of them around just at present; my house had lost the scent of home. Had I had no child, I could've wished she'd remained in the South of the Borough, and let me (quite simply) weigh upon my own inert earth.

Earth myself.

We might even have maintained some sort of friendship, safely founded on distance. But now she was distant and beside me; I looked at her body, it scarcely even lured me, I decided the flesh was too tight about the bone.

(I didn't mean to say it) I said: 'I feel thwarted and trapped.'

Her head drew slightly back. 'You're the prisoner of your own pointlessness. Why not escape to reality?'

I can give you her words, but not her tone. The finer seemed deliberately trying to imitate the coarser, as satinwood may be made to look like bamboo. And the repetition! Not

143

that she *always* said I was lazy, and that that was why I hadn't got on; sometimes she would take quite the contrary point of view : that I hadn't got on, and that that was why I was lazy. All of which I bore in silence, my face neutral, like a negro's.

'How much longer are you going to go on gardening?'

I felt so weary. 'Are you asking me the hour of my death?'

She took in the whole hopelessness of the situation. Why garden? When I could be doing something useful. Like devising slogans to make people go for their holidays in Greece, when they're so much happier on Margate Sands.

'Don't you want to *get* anywhere?'

'I'm happy where I am.'

'How can you be so selfish?'

Except that she said *sell fish*. Don't be sell fish. How dare I garden when I should be thinking of higher things, like money.

She couldn't understand me. 'The ceiling of your ambition,' she said (and it sounded like a prepared statement), 'is low enough to endanger a hibernating hamster.'

She turned her back on me, strolled to the window and looked down on the terrace houses. She (physically) was no larger than a hamster herself; a mere stoat. But that was only the tip of the iceberg on which my ship, with its load of child, had foundered.

I said : 'What you must realise—what I told you from the start—is that there simply *is no money.*'

'But I didn't realise you'd refuse to do anything about it.'

I placed my hands on hers. She glanced at them, not without a mild curiosity, as if she were trying on a pair of workaday gloves.

'Listen,' I said, smiling down at her. 'Shall we buy up the whole street?'

144

She winced. This wasn't a subject for banter. 'What with?' she said, withdrawing her hands from mine.

'Well, one can at least dream of doing it. Dreams don't cost money.'

'They don't make it, either.'

No. Dreams don't make money; not even dreams of making money. On she went and on till I, if not she, gasped for a comma.

'We have a lovely child,' I said.

'Then he deserves some sacrifice.'

'All right. For his sake let us even be nice to one another. You could try to like me, there's something to like in everyone.'

She turned; challenged me with her upturned eyes. 'I could even love you.'

She could even love me. Yes, but never for what I *was*. Only for what I might *do*. (What do you *do*?) If I succeeded—and (with her to help me) I could—she'd love me. Though I'm uncertain whether *me* is the right word. Or *love*, either. What she could 'love' was not-me—a kind of *her*.

I would love her too; find an affinity of obligation. Never have I felt she was no good; like Renaissance poisoners, she doubled as a cook.

'Thank God those tenants have gone,' she said. And her words kicked against the dust-drifts. A piece of plaster fell from the cornice. 'There!'

But, after all, what would you expect? The house was old, it was saying *then* and not *now*. Could I ever learn to share her sweet disgust for those strange rooms, which seemed hollowed out by a hand and a chisel? The house was lost; the search had been called off; you'd expect ivy to grow up the door.

I said: 'Care to make love with me?'

145

She frowned. Shrugged. 'Not to my knowledge. Anyway, we haven't time.'

She was the minutes to my hours; our hands were never long enough together. I so wanted to make love with her; make love with her that I might love her— if love can be made.

Suddenly I felt I was going mad. I blurted—in front of the child!—and I only heard the words when the naked room threw them back at me : 'I can't go on, I can't, do you hear?'

She stared at me. Perhaps half a minute. Then approached. Quite calm. Put her arms round me. Tight. 'You mean you can't go *back*.'

I felt the muscle in her heart. And said : 'It wasn't my idea to buy up the street. It was Bethell's.'

'It was *mine*,' she replied. And her chin dropped soundlessly into her neck.

'The Managing Director wants me in on it.'

'I know.'

'And do you know what that means? More evictions. All along the street. Hello, I'm your new landlord, I trust our relationship will be a harmonious one, there's only one demand we make of you, and that's to get the hell out of here.'

She sighed at the nearest houses to our own. Cemeteries of the living; with a look that the dead have, if the dead be alive. Drudges and mercenaries. Dogs that're half cats. Shrunk limbs and lives, God-abandoned. Then she turned to me.

'We don't live in Hans Christian Andersen, you know; but in plain unchristian reality.'

'Unless those people are allowed to remain, I shall resign from Bethell, and . . .'

'And what? Join the Salvation Army?'

She laughed. Picked up the child. Went over to the window. Showed him the view. Showed the view her laughter.

'It's high time for a bit of saving.'

'Of *course* it's high time! Unless you want the Council to slap a Compulsory Purchase Order on the whole street.'

'They won't,' I said, with the tone of assurance I'd learnt to adopt when in doubt.

'They say they will.'

'What they say and what they do!'

'I've seen the plans,' she said.

A thought appeared: 'You don't mean our house is included in the plan?'

A miniature wave of her fingers took in every structural fault.

I said: 'But surely they'd make an exception?'

'Unfortunately bureaucrats don't like exceptions.'

I took my child's hand. How delicate, as if it'd been a million years in the making. It had! My child, after such waiting, this is where you'll die!

He smiled at me.

His mother smiled too. 'I'm glad there's a limit to what you'll do for the poor.'

'It seems they'll be evicted in any case.'

She heaved a mock-sigh of relief. 'Precisely! You're learning! All you have to ask yourself is this: Do you want the entire street, including our house, to be compulsorily purchased by the Council, who, after leaving it empty for a number of years—God knows why, but they always do—will cart away every brick, even cart away the *earth*, and erect a vertical slum?'

'I imagine the Council could renovate the existing houses at a tenth of the cost.'

'It isn't their money.'

'*And* be giving people what they want.'

'At a tenth of the delay.'

'Well, why don't they do it?'

Because they aren't Bethell. Bethell's interested in people. People! Otherwise it would be out of business.

'You mean interested in making a profit.'

'Look,' she said. 'Without a profit we can't restore our house, we'll just have to wait for the Council to take it over.'

'Q.E.D.'

'C.P.O.'

'What does that stand for?'

'Compulsory Purchase Order.'

I shrugged. 'Well, can you blame them? They want to raise the level of the lower classes.'

'By about a hundred and fifty feet.'

The poor! I felt so sorry for them. Being pushed around. The Council wouldn't even allow them to remain poor: they had to become the needy; then the underprivileged; now, I gather, they're the disadvantaged. But most I was anxious for my child: the house must remain; and he, at all costs, must remain in it.

I went to the window, looked down on my lower-class neighbours. I was lower-class myself. I shared their touch of earth. My wife would say I shared their penury; I was a proletaire—my wealth was in my offspring.

She joined me at the window; curled her lip at the horizon of highrise. Highrise after highrise, crassly infinite, built to the required standard, with no view, except of the next highrise.

Thousands of windows with lace curtains that say 'no'.

Suddenly the sky was lightened to concrete and the earth to asphalt. Monostructures, megastructures, cellular agglomerates. Too large for man, too small. With clip-on components, plug-in accessories. Images of efficiency, not efficient. The life-world supplanted by a mathematically substructed garb of idealities. The untidy facts adapting themselves to the order which the Council imposed on them. No darksome paths. Enough grass to keep off.

Highrise! I preferred the low crumble of houses with gardens of rough rye grass, where boys can take their bicycles to bits, and put them together again. Walls of valerian and convolvulus, and fences of old doors.

Neighbours! I prayed no one would release them from their cells, knowing (even then) the old lag's fear of freedom. Prison becomes home, identified by smell, the stink of urine, heavier than air. Waiting rooms. What're they waiting for? What do they do?

(Such madness!) I suddenly felt sorry for my wife. 'You'd rather be among the Rolls-Royces,' I said.

'Even if they're owned by the wrong people.'

'It's a terrible life.'

'One day,' she mused, 'we'll see the Rolls-Royces in our street.' Her interest in it was speculative. Whereas the Council's was cadastral. Mine: charismatic.

Mine didn't count.

I said : 'Can't the people stay?'

She looked along the crumble of roofs. 'Do you believe they want to?'

'Will children thank you for removing them from their mother? Try saying: Your mother's a bully, we'll board you with God at the Ritz.'

'And the Ritz would stink to high heaven.'

'Of course. That's their way of re-creating their one-room world.'

Funny how I thought of tenants as children. More beetles than ladybirds, whom flowers lure less than the dung heap. Such breeders of junk! Because with junk you can do things, it does things for you.

I missed my children. Poor children! Society is divided;

149

and if you divide a sum so complex as society, you'll be left
with a remainder. Never will they qualify for accommodation
in one of those new blocks. Or 'prisons', as the ungrateful
inmates call them. Doesn't each unit have its water closet?
Eliminate the shit, lest it enrich the earth. Learn to hate shit,
and ye shall see shit in everything. Daisies're shit, the
municipal grass is purged of daisies. Old houses're shit
because they have no water closets; and if they have water
closets they're still shit because they're old.

A bus passed.

Does your butcher sell Paris fashions?

Harrods.

Is your cook a concocter of poisons?

CHAPTER XV

'Lots of flags flying,' said the Managing Director.

'What?'

'Houses for sale. More boards around than at any time since the wreck of the Spanish Armada.'

I would buy up the street before Bethell did. Not the whole of it, at least not all at once, I'd start with a single house, tell the tenants they wouldn't be thrown out; and make it clear to Bethell that I wouldn't be bought out.

Having no money to speak of, I tried the Societies, you can imagine their answer, they never got as far as a survey, which was just as well, they charge £45 for a half-hour survey.

'But why don't you mortgage your own house?' they said.

'Would you mortgage your own child?'

I was already despairing when I happened to see a poster offering 100% mortgages. No name. Just a number, which I at once 'phoned, asking them if they would grant a mortgage on a going concern. They said indeed they would, this was their speciality. So I paid their investigation fee of £50. Three months later they said they were sorry, I wasn't credit-worthy. (I gathered afterwards they have no funds to lend: they earn their living from the investigation fees.)

I won't weary you with my whole catalogue of mistakes—except, of course, that they could be a warning if you decided to follow me into property; in which case I suggest you write to me, HM Prisons.

In the end I did something I vowed I never would: I invited my Bank Manager to lunch. If he asked for security . . .

But the question was never raised. What would be raised was the interest—till it almost equalled the rent. I was embarking on my new career as an unpaid employee of the bank.

I view a house of sorts, the vendor offered to give the tenants notice. Poor tenants! It's about the only notice anyone ever takes of them. I (obviously) said no. It was a going concern, wasn't it?

I didn't trouble with surveyors, I could see the place was a shambles. So were the tenants: storemen; rag-and-bone men; and (ironically) dustmen. Dust everywhere. It gathered in wads, like shearings from mangy sheep. A carpet of dust half-covered the linoleum, and over it a baby crawled, his mother let him, he had no father, there were men around, but no father.

My wife came round to inspect.

'Tenants're vermin,' she said.

'Why must you keep saying they're vermin?'

'The house stinks.'

'Precisely! It's the house that stinks, not the tenants.'

We had trouble getting into rooms, most of the tenants being in bed. (I've never—regardless of the the time of day— been into a house of bedsits when most of the tenants weren't in bed.)

I told my new tenants I'd have to put the rent up, whereupon they went to the Rent Tribunal, who reduced it. The house was now running at a loss, so back to my Bank Manager, who let me have all I asked for— these being the years, you may remember, when Britain was going to borrow itself rich. The banks, with government approval, were lending hundreds of thousands of pounds to people who weren't worth so many pence, and whose experience scarcely exceeded my own. But after two years came the squeeze, and many of them found a friend in the Official Receiver.

Only a few doors further along the street were TWO ADJOINING INVESTMENT PROPERTIES SUITABLE FOR HORIZONTAL CONVERSION. Full vacant possession, so no question of evicting anyone; that had already been done. (Why, incidentally, do agents say *full* when they mean *empty?*)

My wife discovered who the vendor was and wrote to him direct—on Bethell's headed paper. An appointment for 8 a.m. sharp, if you please. She was even early, but he was already waiting on the steps. 'This is my husband, I thought I'd bring him along.'

For a moment he was silent, looking at her with mystified contempt, as if she were a modern picture, and he couldn't be certain which was her right way up. Then : 'I was expecting you to be a man,' he said.

'I'm sorry,' she snorted, 'but there's nothing I can do about *that*. Not even to please *you*.' She was excellent at this sort of work; her histrionic nastiness was always utterly convincing.

(In two minds) 'Well,' he said, rather distantly, 'would you like to . . .'

He was apparently expecting her to walk away.

'How much're you asking?'

He smiled. 'So you're interested. Have the agents been told you're here?'

'Not by me.'

'Don't. In that case I can let you have it for £19,950.'

'It's extremely generous of you not to charge £20,000.'

He shrugged. 'Make it twenty if you like.'

Casually (almost as if doodling) her fingers glanced at the crumble on the portico, picked at it delicately until a piece of

153

stucco fell, a little avalanche, breaking against the penitential steps.

'Please!' he said. 'Careful!'

'I shall be!' she retorted, looking up at the Corinthian cauliflowers as if expecting them to pollinate over her hair.

I said: 'Why don't we go inside, as the gentleman suggests?'

'Penknife?' she replied.

He frowned at each of us in turn.

I said I never carried one.

'Mistake,' she said. Her hand felt in her large leather bag, her eyes were still surveying the hundred-year-old stucco, her hand seemed to act independently of her. Presently it emerged with a pair of scissors, tiny nail scissors, they began attacking the sides of the hole which her fingers had already made in the hundred-year-old stucco. Till an entire brick was bared.

'Brick!' she exclaimed, as if the porticos of North Kensington should've been made of solid steel.

'Well?'

She ignored him. She was now scraping at the mortar, if it could still be called mortar, she would doubtless call it *powder*, for it *powdered* into her dress, she made a great to-do of brushing off the *powder*.

He said he was sorry; not sarcastically, I don't think he said it sarcastically. He then enquired: 'Are you a . . . qualified surveyor?'

Hell, the snort-at-him! Did he flinch? I don't know, but suddenly he—it was so odd—he paled: as if those little puffs of breath that darted from her nostrils were scissor-points, aimed at his eyes. The fear in them! There's something fearful about fear, I was afraid he might crumble, like that hundred-year-old stucco.

She observed him, said: 'You needn't be a surveyor to tell what's wrong with *your* house.'

'It's a very nice house,' he said quietly. Who *was* she? She'd written to him on Bethell paper. Vendors are usually prepared to drop the price if they're dealing with a firm.

'Then would you care to . . . show us over . . . Buckingham Palace?'

The blood that had left his cheeks now suddenly flowed back. 'Look here, madam! I never said my house was a palace. Did I ever say my house was a palace?'

'No, no,' she replied. 'And it isn't the cottage of Little Red Riding Hood, either. It's a dangerous structure. I'm not going inside. I can see what's needed, one would have to start again from scratch, cost as much as a new house, plus a thousand for demolition.'

'Are you a buyer?' he enquired. 'Or just out for a day's sight-seeing?'

'I'll offer you ten,' she replied, opening her bag and replacing the scissors.

But it was no use, she'd over-played, under-offered, 'Good day,' he said; his back turned round to face us, he muttered as he went.

'If you're as unpleasant as that,' I said, 'no wonder he won't do business with you.'

'Wait and see.'

I waited. We didn't see him, though. Nor did he write; telephone. Nothing.

Next month the For Sale board came down, I assumed he'd found a buyer, but then we received particulars of an auction, apparently he couldn't face the thought of showing his house to anyone else.

'I'll try putting in a bid,' I said; 'how much do you think it's worth?'

She shrugged. 'Seventeen. Maybe eighteen.'

155

'Well, how high do I go?'

'Leave that to me.'

The property boys were there, about twenty or thirty of them, no one else, I could tell them by their light-weight overcoats, belts undone, I could've told them in the bath.

The auctioneer shouted through a microphone, complained he was hoarse, I'm not surprised. Could we please make the bidding brisk, he doubted if his voice would hold.

The bidding began at £5,000. The usual mini-gestures, invisible to the non-professional, raised it by hundreds to £7,200.

Then it hesitated.

'This is ridiculous,' shouted the auctioneer, 'the bidding doesn't hesitate at £7,200, not for a house that's neighbour to the manor of North Kensington.'

Neighbour to my arse.

Then my wife stood up, yes, she *stood up*, she already *stood out*, a woman amongst all those property boys, and wearing white mink, a present from her father, it had something to do with tax.

She was looked at, of course. With curiosity. But not the curiosity of lust. Resentment, rather. Auctions were for the pro. If they became a pastime for women of leisure . . .

'Ten thousand,' she said.

The auctioneer stared. Had he misheard?

'No, you didn't mishear,' she said.

'But madam, the last bid was £7,200.'

'The last bid was ten thousand.'

'But . . .'

'Do get on.'

Murmurs. Sit down, you silly bitch.

The auctioneer recovered his former hoarseness. 'That was a lesson from the lady.'

His eyes scanned us for the bidding.

'£10,100.'

It had resumed, silent, and (as far as one could see) invisible.

Another hesitation, so he looked around, arms urgently raised, and turned again to my wife. 'Well, madam?'

'Thirteen thousand,' she said.

Men groaned, chairs grated, and on all sides Jesus wept. *Stay*, begged the auctioneer, a very Christ of suffering, he too almost wept. But the hammer came down as it had to, because they were all wasting their fucking time.

The Managing Director of Bethell congratulated me on my wife's brilliance, as a result of which, he assured me, I should make a real kill. They'd already, as a matter of fact, converted some similar houses, so perhaps I'd care to make use of their plans.

Before I could convert, I had to ask my Bank Manager for a further loan, but he said I must be under some misapprehension. 'It's you who're banking with us, not we with you.' Bethell, however, were a friend in need: they would acquire my indebtedness to the bank in return for my property; and in case they hadn't made themselves a thousand per cent clear . . .

No, I wouldn't make over Chivalry House.

They hastened to add that this was a mere formality, because they had no intention of ousting me, heaven forbid, indeed I could remain there all my life.

'All my life?' I said. 'That's not long enough.'

'You're pressing a very hard bargain. Well, then: you and your heirs for ever.'

So why did they want it? Something to do with tax?

When I told my wife I'd refused their offer, her face dropped as far as Knightsbridge, and the next moment it was hateful with a new intensity. This was the beginning of the kill.

She cried, took the child in her arms, he cried too. (She wanted to know) what was the *matter* with me? I could never see a silver lining but I was looking for a dark cloud to go with it. 'Look, the child's crying too,' she moaned.

It was like a Polish funeral.

She blew her nose. 'What do you think is going to *happen* to us?'

'You'll find me in the garden,' I said.

Get away from her, then she'd stop.

'Garden,' she sobbed. 'What tense are you living in?'

'Don't,' I said; 'we have a child.'

'I wouldn't have known!'

'Please!'

'I'm going to have a nervous breakdown,' she said, as if it were something she owed herself.

Again I made the mistake of pleading with her. She only screamed the more. But how was I to calm her? If only there were still bed; body to body I could no longer love her; and if I put out my hand to touch her, she flinched from me as if eggshell.

That night I had a wet dream, and she was furious; she wouldn't have *minded* if I'd been out with a *soubrette*, that's something she could understand from a creature like *me*; but apparently I'd rather make love with *no one* than make love with *her*. So why didn't I just *clear off*? Clear off with my *soubrette. Clear off!* She wanted a man in her bed.

Then she went back to her plate-throwing. But she didn't throw them at the floor, or at the walls; she threw them at *me*. 'You're not a *man*!' she screamed.

No, I was a coconut shy.

And in front of the child, too.

So I ran out, I thought it was the decent thing to do.

158

Decency is weakness.

And went to Bethell. Signed. Signed away Chivalry House.

My wife, I've told you, had made a scene in front of the child, but you can't really blame her, it was her only way of averting disaster. Yes, we were now solvent. And even if my child wasn't to inherit the house, he'd at least live there, and meantime he'd have peace from screams. Or so I hoped. But she continued.

I pleaded with her. 'Is the child to be a war baby?'

'I never wanted war,' she said.

No. She wanted victory. And I thought she'd won, but she was to drive me out.

And out I went. For an hour. For a day. She wanted me out for ever.

That took her more than a *blitzkrieg*: it was *guerre à l'outrance*. And I still carry that war in my heart. A world war. Her smallness was without limit. When I hear of skies being scraped, it's of her I think. But even that gives no notion, for a teaspoonful of her would weigh millions of tons, there was enough of her to deaden the earth. I feared being crushed by the fall of one hair from her head. Her atoms were packed so tight that you could hardly get a finger between them—as if a whole moon of her were packed into one Tokyo Tube.

So small, where was she not? She was DDT in the sky over India; she was cadmium in the kidneys of the Japanese; it would be impossible to take a sample from any of the world's oceans without finding measurable quantities of her.

Once she'd seemed so the right size. But now she was frighteningly big, or nauseatingly small. She and I weren't even the same species. I would rather have fucked cattle. She was her father, magnified, the streets she trod were ants' paths; and she didn't even keep to them—took short cuts

159

across houses, flattening roofs into cellars, people fled like bugs.

There was no beauty in her anger; it wasn't (no, no) the foam on the waves of the storm, but the foam on the lips of an epileptic.

'What a father! You've even sold the roof over his head!'

'Your idea.'

'Imagine what's become of us when it's better to sell the roof that's over his head.'

His eyes asked when a crane would come along and lift it off.

'We'll manage,' I said.

'Manage what? You aren't capable of managing a barrow. Why don't you just leave us? In peace. What use are you? We're better off without you. The door's open. Like Dr Barnardo's.'

'You need a holiday,' I said. Why couldn't *she* go away? Round the world. And round.

Then a further short altercation, lasting little less than three quarters of an hour. I shan't give you it verbatim, or any other of her rows, there was a routine about our inferno. Why bore you? All unhappy marriages are the same; it's only happy ones that achieve the variety of things positive. I myself have tried to forget. Alas, I have a tolerably good memory, as sieves go.

And my child whimpering in the corner, like a dog that's hit.

I went out. Suddenly I felt ill. But never mind, my wife wouldn't scream as long as I was out. I would stay out till the child was asleep, I committed adultery for want of anything better to do—returning on tip-toe, only to hear the door rasp at me in the anger of broken sleep.

Next morning my child asked me why I hadn't read to

160

him. I said I would read to him now. But somehow it had to be the evening.

I saw the doctor. 'Doctor, my skin is taut across the forehead. My brain is clogged with catarrh.'

'There's no physical cause.'

'Yes, there is : my wife.'

Not every day was a screaming one. Some were silent—white and insufferable. And my nights were dreams that I was already at breakfast, trapped in snow, the only sound was the turning of *The Times*, it was thunder; and the pouring of Kellog's Cornflakes—it was an avalanche.

I went into the garden, cried among my plants, and if my eyes were dry it wasn't because I was happy but because I'd hardened my heart.

With a hard heart maybe I could get by.

At night, awake, I address myself in the past imperative, tell myself not to have got caught up. I don't like blondes, I've never liked blondes, that's why I didn't get caught up. But I did. No, I need sleep, I must go on telling myself I didn't get caught up. I need sleep. I need sleep to not-know I got caught up. But sleep, when it comes, is like waking.

I wake. With a mouthful of nylon. I did get caught up. Nearly-didn't won't help. I recall critical moments, the recall is as concrete as a dream, it ceases to be recall, I mean it loses the inflection that says *past*, so that *then* becomes *now*. But gradually I return to clock and calendar, to my child's making and unmaking. My mistakes recede, recede towards me, grow larger, louder, blonder, memory maddens into the now-here. While the world around me is a whisper and pale blue.

'I need a holiday,' I said.

'You need a day's work. Get out and work.'

She didn't mean get out in the garden, the garden wasn't out, the garden wasn't work, a fact which she emphasised with a further throwing of plates. Perhaps it would relieve her feelings. It did. For she could then say, quite calmly: 'You're a man for whom I have the opposite of respect. You're worthless. Worse than worthless.'

What was I, then? Fuel for her machine. Fuel is something you consume, you turn it into energy, and it's no longer there.

My child cries beyond all consolation, I must go out, under the circumstances it's the only decent thing to do. I must go out. See a solicitor. I already had a wife. I now have two people against me.

'You must leave her,' he says, thinking of my own interests without regard to his own pocket.

'I can't.'

'I've known too many cases of this kind. *You can't not.*'

'And break my child's home?'

'It's broken already.'

Maybe he was right. Can two walk together, except they be agreed?

Should I take my child away? *Right* away. To some island where metal was unknown; where there were no speed limits—where there was no speed to limit; where I could build a new house and tend a new garden.

But he wouldn't come. And I wouldn't go. He would rather stay with his mother, just as I, who was used to London, would never exchange its ton of grime for any pastoral paradise that Keats might sing, or Claude paint. I was hooped to where I planted.

'Another day!'

Those were her first words on waking. Her only pleasure came from the enactment of her misery. 'You want to kill me,' she said. And her eyes were as bitter as rattlesnakes, they had teeth, and her mouth too.

'Don't talk like that in front of the child.'

162

Her nails were at me. 'You coward! You break my nerves, I was never like this before you came along, and you haven't even the mercy to kill me.'

'I'll kill you then.'

With inchoate fury she reached the high yellow note, she screamed things I've chosen not to remember, and things I chose not to hear. You'll never (I hope) hear a mother scream like my dead wife. But the eyes of children whose homes are within the roar of factories, the roar of gunfire, the roar of roars, are known to you, if only from TV. Poor children, I pity them all. But to see the maiming of your own child, it was like the paralysis of someone you've loved in the flesh.

Suddenly I said: 'Why don't you go? With the child, if you like. I'll see him at weekends, he can come and stay with me.'

Her counsel was to bring that up in court, being a measure of my love for the child.

I caught his twitch, and at night I had convulsions, which shook my whole earth. All night my head was an uproar of thoughts, the world was flat, and I was falling off the edge of it, I was falling off the edge of myself.

And in the morning her screams returned.

'What's the point?' I said. 'You can't make me unhappier than I am.' (How wrong I was!)

I recalled our first weeks—when not to see her for twelve hours was pain. And now, were we cast on a desert island, I'd trade her for one long-playing disc.

And still we were in each other's arms. But struggling; wrestling; boxing; I don't say the fault wasn't partly mine; but she took an eye for a tooth.

Marriage!—mutually assured destruction; best known by its acronym, MAD.

She's dead now; the funeral's over, and the undertakers have lit their cigarettes. But I still feel myself at war, and at war I shall remain till the world's last quarter of an hour.

What escape had I? I'd even renounced adultery, a week of organisation for one quick fuck. My fucks henceforth were in the mind, the inner emigration. I touched my child. My plants. Touched them in a wild smother of affection.

'I want a divorce,' she said.

'I believe you.'

She wanted a divorce from all that's good, humane, and natural. I had such hate of her. She was a swollen lump inside me. I was hate-sick. I carried her photograph in my notecase, took it out and looked at it when she became too much to bear; held it at arm's length, she was out there.

'I want a divorce,' she insisted.

'We have a child, there *is* no divorce.'

'Child! What's the child to *you*? Was it from *your* loins he came?'

'Without me you could never have done it.'

She stared at me in astonishment, as if the very soil had risen in rebellion against those who were accustomed to tread it. 'Oh! I underestimated you! The outsize impertinence! You place *that* beside nine months of travail! Now you've measured your care for him!'

'He's my child too,' I said.

'*Your* child! Your toy, you mean. Do your populating elsewhere!'

I hated her. Her intonation. The tone of her eyes. So schooled in bitterness, she was the very Christ of hate. If, therefore, gentle reader, thou art a woman and a wise one, take counsel of her, I prithee, how thy man may best be hurt: shoot not in every part, but seek thou with diligence where he most abhorreth the points of thy barbs; and thither alone let them fly.

To thy heart's content.

Myself, I had one particularly sensitive spot; my father-hood. As soon as she discovered this, she stopped calling me arrogant, self-doubting, butterfly, recluse, misogynist, womaniser, fascist, leftie; and insisted I had no fatherly affection.

Then how did she explain my living with her? Did she think I enjoyed her company? I'd prefer the work-house, or the open road. Sleep rough in my old gardener's arms.

'Why don't you go out?' she said. 'It's raining hard.'

The perpetual sarcasm. You'll say I'm sarcastic myself. It was from her I learnt it.

'Go!' she said.

But I must find a means of staying. Preserve my inner darkness. It was prison. All right, the thing about prison is that you don't leave. The same as my tenants. Not unless you're evicted by the bailiff. You learn to endure the no breath of air. The only air is breath. You drink it. It tastes like other people's urine.

I might learn to like it.

'You're a shit!' she said.

Always shit. Shit was ugh! The ultimate hate.

I shan't leave her, though, I shan't divorce her. Our hate was already *nisi* and absolute. I'll stay—wish her womb would rise into her throat, that it had choked her at birth, and then my child would never have sickened into life.

'You aren't still here?' she screamed.

We can't separate. We can't. I feared it like an operation I'd already been through.

She picked up a doll which my child had had as a baby, he'd started playing with it again. She picked it up and hurled it at the floor, crushed it with her high heel, kicked it against the wall, it whirled over and over.

I felt faint, my head was like a car chase, we were on crashward course, and I knew it.

Suddenly my body, without my telling it, got up, and left the house.

And my child in a palsy of nerves.

CHAPTER XVI

I was madly happy, from prison released, no careful adultery, but days and nights of fullest nakedness, indoors and out, venting months of stored-up sperm and care. With women who even quite liked me; licked the last drops from me, or from the grass on which they fell.

I dreamt my wife didn't exist; that I'd dreamt her. Tore up all the old photographs, each time a kind of murder.

Then the hunt for an Earls Court room, only in Earls Court will you find tins of soup for one, and may you buy a single egg.

The South Kensington Accommodation Bureau, affectionately known as Skab, were pleased to see an English face, they should have no difficulty in finding me something. 'Are you married or single?'

'Yes,' I said.

(Glancing up from the form) 'Which?'

'Married. I mean single.'

'Well, make up your mind.'

They found me a room in one of those houses where there're an awful lot of things you're not allowed to do. Antimacassars were provided. Indeed everything about it was anti. Luxury bedsit, it was called—which means a shower and kitchenette behind a partition, and you must be double-jointed to get into them.

Newly converted. Already frayed.

'What do you *do*?' enquired the large-breasted land-lady.

'Do? I'm a gentleman.'

'Ah. We've had gentlemen before and they've been very happy.'

The bathroom was bigger than the kitchenette, yet not big enough for a bath.

Showers I hate.

She called my room a flat. It was a flat, she explained, because the door had a lock.

'Don't lock yourself out.'

I locked myself out. She had to come and let me in.

'Are you a family man?'

'No,' I said; 'I'm a broken family man.'

She asked me to share her suet roll; said it was too much for her. By God it was too much! You sank your teeth into it and sent for help to get out. And tapioca pudding; get stuck into it and you'll never be heard of again.

One of the other tenants invites me for biscuits and cocoa. 'Marriage bust up?'

'Yes.'

'Messy.'

Where, I wondered, was my child? At home? Or did my wife take him with her to the office? I hated to think of him fauntleroying with tycoons.

I spoke to him on the telephone, he sounded all right, I went straight round and saw him, he smiled, not broadly, but with deep inner joy. I felt consoled, though undeserving.

His mother supposed I'd like a cup of coffee.

'Yes, please.'

'You've got a nerve.'

Not for months had she been so pleasant.

We could be friends. We could've been friends without

separating, I was insufficiently flower-giving, compliment-paying.

'Do you mind if I take some of my things?'

She shook her head. 'Take your bits of wreckage.'

'Thank you,' I said. 'And the cat to keep me company.'

'But I don't want you hanging around, I've got a lot to do, you can take the child out.'

But I wanted to be with him *here*. He brought me his drawings of houses, 'You've forgotten to put in the windows,' I said. 'Oh,' he said.

'They're quite good, nonetheless.'

He liked the *quite good*. Very good would mean very good for a child, but quite good meant quite good by any standard.

I taught him to make a mouse from a handkerchief.

'Stroke it,' I said.

He stroked it.

'Time for a little mouse to say good night.'

But it jumped out of my hand, onto his lap.

He laughed.

Then he pulled its tail, and once again it was a handkerchief.

'Poor mouse!'

He nestled against me, he was a mouse himself.

'Let's go out,' I suggested.

'No!'

I thought he said it for the struggle, to be chased, to be seized.

So I chased him, seized him.

But he didn't laugh. And when we reached the door, he held the jamb as if I would take him away for ever.

'No, *no*!'

He was screaming, kicking. His mother wondered what the matter was.

'I can't force him,' I said.

F*   169

'Do you want me to help you?' she retorted.

So I wrested his fists from the jamb, he was so strong, I was so weak.

Within minutes he was laughing again.

I saw him every day. Every day I had to wrest his fists from the jamb.

And every day I went back to my bedsit; to its stillness, more distracting than any sound; to the *Why, dear God*!

For hours I prayed; at least knelt.

I 'phoned my wife. 'Should I stop seeing the child? Save the tension?'

'No, he can't spend the whole day indoors.'

'But . . . if *you* take him out . . .'

'With me he's the same.'

'You mean . . .'

'Yes, and when I take him to the office he huddles under my chair, holding onto my skirt.'

'I don't believe you! You're trying to hurt me!'

'Ask Bethell.'

'My poor child, what does he say?'

'Nothing. Except at night. He wakes up and cries for you.'

'O God!'

I collected my few things, I was round at once, hugged him with a passionate, furious care. 'Don't worry, I'm back, I'm back for ever, I'll put you into your bed in the evening, and you'll see me in mine in the morning.'

My wife overheard me.

'Nothing of the kind!' she said.

I was unpacking my things. 'What did you say?'

'Without so much as asking!'

'But you see how things are.'

'Yes. Haven't you done enough damage?'

'Of *course* it's enough.'

'Then get out.'

170

'I can't.'

'Can't you?'

(The old sarcasm) and suddenly she seized my pocket-watch, I was just unpacking it, I'd had it for centuries, I felt I'd had it almost as long as my child, and she hurled it at the door.

I nearly died.

'Get out!'

Yes, I must get out for the child's sake, I picked up my watch, put it to my ear, its heart had stopped.

I staggered down the path, banging my shin against the pedal of my old bike, moaned down the street, had stitch, felt broken in the middle. 'My child!' I kept saying, over and over, like a monk's *Lord have mercy*, till at last it's in the head without a word.

Next day I was feverish, my shit was urine, my urine was blood. Nothing seemed left inside me, except worry. I was inside *it*.

At night, sleepless, I hugged my cat; swore I would never ride to hounds, I never had. Would let the wasps share my breakfast marmalade. I would even shut doors with care, for the doors' sake, knowing that the displacement of one atom could hurt my child, and even shook the stars.

I telephoned my wife, arranged to see her in the evening.

She was alone in the drawing-room, no light on, she looked so small in it, it was much too large for one person.

'Is the child asleep?' I said.

She shrugged.

I crept into the nursery. Do you know anything more beautiful than a child asleep? Every night in my cell I imagine I can creep into his nursery and see him asleep.

Back in the drawing-room. The outline of her body hadn't moved. Even her head was at the same downcast angle. Do you know?—and for this if nothing else I deserve to be in prison—I pitied her. I had pitied Mussolini when I saw a photograph of his dejection in captivity. I would have pleaded for him, even if he'd never made the trains run on time.

My wife had made the trains run on time.

Can't I comfort her? Perhaps there's a curative mud that'll draw out the corrupted juices of her body.

I switched on the table lamp. Her face was like a thousand sleepless nights.

She got up, I followed her to the kitchen, where she poured herself a whisky and soda, then leant against the 'fridge, she would make a friend of it in her misery.

She felt for a cigarette. Lit it from the toaster.

Then suddenly (imagine my astonishment!) she turned to me, wordless, flung her arms round my neck, as if they were words; they were. She sobbed onto my shoulder, 'The silence! The silence!' I took her in my arms, I was all pity, pity, and (God forgive me!) desire too; as if I'd never before touched her.

Could my child walk in and see us? Shall I call him? Never mind the tears, we were together. What if, as with some mothers, she ill-fed him, neglected his teeth or ears, went out and left him unattended? But she hadn't.

I said to her : 'Every article in every magazine is about the children of broken homes; every snatch of overheard conversation.'

She released herself from my arms, drifted back into the drawing-room. 'I'm sorry about your cares. What about mine?'

'Exactly, I understand them.'

'The silence!'

'Then have me back. You can try. You must.'

'No.'

172

'I'm sick. Can't you see? Do you expect me to be away and well?'

'You should've thought of that before.'

'Let's go the theatre; a film.'

'No.'

'Dine out; dance.'

'No.'

I went on, though to say no was her only pleasure. Not the tender kind of no, the no that puts its arms round you. But a no that's chopped to the bone, it's the first two letters of not.

Like shot.

Pull the trigger and out it comes.

Did she expect me to be away and well? I should've thought of that before.

Did I hope to play on her pity? I was giving her the pleasure of saying no.

(The moral turpitude!) I pitied her, it was a holiday from hate. Hatred is a thing you have to work at. Does God keep a part-time hell?

'Go!' she said. And the anger-vein stood out on her forehead.

So I went. With a ton of iron inside me.

I could hardly walk. In Kensington High, noisy and noxious, I felt faint, I mustn't faint with the child to see.

'Come every day,' he'd said.

'Yes.'

'Promise?'

'Promise.'

My wife wanted me to have him for the weekend, he and I slept head-and-tail in one three-foot bed.

'How old are you?' he enquired, bouncing into my one chair.

'A thousand million years.'

'I hope you live another thousand million.'

'Do you?'

'That'll make you two thousand million years old.'

'What a lot of candles!'

I didn't say I hoped he lived twice that long, for children believe they're immortal. Are.

'Have you got a ball?' he said.

'What?'

'B.A.L.L.'

We strolled into Hyde Park, played catch, then took a boat on the Serpentine, I taught him to row, I hadn't rowed since Oxford. Come forward! Are you ready? Paddle! Easy oar! Drop! Yes, I remembered the words of command, he was impressed, so was I.

Then he had a fizzy drink, the idea of a fizzy drink is to shake it vigorously and then let it shoot up.

He said: 'Look! The flowers on the grass are like candles on a cake.'

I rather liked that.

CHAPTER XVII

My wife was taking me to court, I'd paid her no maintenance.

(Decency is weakness) I'd paid her in cash, I deliberately didn't pay her by cheque, I didn't want to demean her, you see.

I'd paid her no maintenance!

I went back to my solicitor, swore an affidavit, channelled my payments through his office. (More expense.)

'You aren't leaving very much for yourself, you know.'

It was good of him to show me such concern. I don't think he was in doubt whether I'd be able to pay him.

'There's my directorship of Bethell.'

'Can they dismiss you?'

'They wouldn't.'

'We don't know.'

'They've treated me very generously.'

'How so?'

'Got me out of debt.'

'Did they ask for any favour in return?'

'I transferred my houses into their name.'

'Including Chivalry House?'

'Yes.'

He drew in a breath as if it were a balloon to be filled; then let it out again. 'The deal, unless I'm mistaken, didn't pass through my hands.'

175

'No, I . . .'

'You thought you'd . . . save unnecessary expense.'

'I felt I'd already been troubling you more than I should.'

He smiled. 'Do you know the price of developable land in North Kensington?'

I think in fact I did. Vaguely. Not that I'd ever cared about it. The average was £90,000 per acre. The house had three acres and more. You can work it out.

'But this,' I said, 'is rather hypothetical. No development is possible. Part of the agreement was that I should be free to live there as long as I liked.'

'But you *don't* live there.'

'My son does. And his posterity shall. It's all in the agreement.'

Again the balloon filled; and emptied. 'They can only remain as long as it stands.'

'It stands as long as they remain.'

'Does the agreement stipulate that Bethell are to maintain it in good repair?'

'It's implied.'

'Then we're at the mercy of Bethell's inferences.'

'You mean they'll let it crumble.'

He raised his hands interrogatively. He was no seer. And I, for that matter, was no lawyer. 'In future you'd better . . .'

'Yes, yes. But tell me the worst that can happen.'

'Quite simple: the Health Department declares it uninhabitable; the Borough Surveyor declares it dangerous.'

'Then what am I to do?'

'Is the house listed?'

'Listed?'

'Of architectural interest.'

'It's considered a monstrosity.'

'That's not a known impediment.'

176

Meantime there was the matter of my wife's petition. Back to my solicitor. Had my family fought on William's right flank or his left? They fought for Harold, I said. Ah. He had to know this, at ten pounds an hour, so as to brief my counsel; with whom he arranged a conference.

At the hearing before the Registrar in Somerset House, my wife complained that what I paid her was not commensurate with my earnings. The complaint was dismissed on the grounds that the husband had to have something to live on, a judgement which my wife's counsel appealed against.

(More expense) a hearing in the High Court. His lordship asked me if I was able to increase the maintenance. I assured him I could double it if only my wife would consent to my living with her. Her counsel was appalled at my suggestion, and (having never met me in his life) vouched for the un-endurability of my behaviour, vouched for it at such length that the Judge had to remind him that his client was appealing for more maintenance, not suing for divorce. Although the appeal was dismissed, costs were awarded against me, and bills arrived with an alacrity for which the general procedures of the legal profession had hardly prepared me.

I must find work—to feed lawyers who want to deprive my child of his father. I must find work—not work in my garden, but where my child can feel no oneness.

One day, when I called at the house to collect him, my wife said he couldn't see me. You already know what followed: I told you on page one or so, and I'm not going to tread the same ground again. Not because I'm afraid of boring you, for you're doubtless bored already, this is a father's tale, you'd like it to be a mother's. No, it's just that I want to save myself the pain. In fact I would never have started on this accursed book if one of the warders hadn't suggested it.

'Go on,' he said, 'it'll take your mind off prison.'

177

'And when it's finished?'

'Try sending it to a publisher.'

Others made less cordial suggestions.

I said : 'I can't write. I've never written. I wouldn't know where to begin.'

'At the beginning?'

Beginning. There's no such thing. I began, you remember, at the beginning of the end. That, you see, was all I intended to write about, but then I found myself having to explain how my wife and I met, and I've been going on from there.

Damn, I put down my pen and can't find it, I'm always losing my pen, though it's practically my only possession, that and a bottle of ink, I like the flow, it sometimes blots, I don't mind blots, the pen is somehow *me*, a thing of nature, while the sheet, though it may once have been wood, is now an inorganic article, a blot won't hurt, in fact I blot each new sheet on purpose.

Hell, that's the second time I've put down my pen and lost it! Do you know I almost *cried*.

Where was I? My wife said I couldn't see the child. But (you remember?) I took him regardless.

She retaliated by ringing 999. That worked awfully well, the Bobby broke up the only party I gave in my luxury bedsit. I had shaken the dehydrated minestrone into the boiling water; it had risen like Japanese flowers—while my friends (friends?) said the right things, had I made it myself?

I was arrested. She got me arrested. And a man who's arrested obviously shouldn't see his child. So she took out a court injunction.

A Judge of the Family Division—yes, Family Division, I think I've got the name right—forbade me in his kind and usual way to have any contact with my child until the matter was investigated by a Court Welfare Officer.

178

There is still, I gather—and I hope hereby to put this to rights—the odd mother who remains ignorant of the power with which the law invests her: if she wants to stop her husband from seeing the children, she only has to bring some charge against him, for instance that he wanted to visit them when they were ill. It's perfectly simple, she doesn't even have to provide any evidence that she's speaking the truth, in fact a lie will do equally well.

Next day my child didn't see me. What did he think? I telephoned the High Court. When would I see the Welfare Officer?

The Welfare Officer? She's—I must realise—frightfully overworked, they sound surprised at my expressing no sympathy for her.

Each day I telephoned. Each day I listened for the telephone.

It was a month before she came, I must be glad, because most people wait twice that long, I must be glad that most people wait twice that long.

'Good morning,' she said. She made it sound like a weather forecast. And on entering my bedsit—it was decidedly an entrance—she bestowed on me a very slight bow, as if adjusting her stomach.

Don't Judges bow on entering the court?

She'd already had a long chat with my wife.

I was the person my wife had told her about.

The interrogation began. Had I *realise*d what I was *doing* when I *grabbed the child*?

I said the effect could've been harmful.

She assured me it was harmful, she'd seen his twitch, and this had commenced on the very next day.

The very next day?

My wife had told her so.

'She's a liar,' I said.

What a novice I am! I should realise the only way a husband can assuage the anger of the law is by swearing his wife's a saint.

'Liar?' she gasped.

I'd condemned myself out of my own mouth.

Unfair Officer! Maybe in fifty years I'll look on her objectively; camera-cool. I hope not.

I said: 'Did you ask my child?'

'He said the same.'

'I suppose you asked him in front of his mother.'

She glared, as if it were not she but her profession that was being questioned.

'I interviewed them separately.'

'My poor child!'

'Poor child indeed! Didn't you say the effect of your grabbing him could be harmful?'

I made matters worse by answering: 'It was not a choice of harm or no harm, but a choice between harms.'

'What was the other harm, may I ask?'

(She actually had to ask.)

'The harm of not seeing his father.'

'That's for the court to decide.'

'All right. Let the court decide. But when? Can I count on a hearing this week?'

I shall never forget her look of outrage at my suggestion that the court might act quickly. I'd criticised *her*, I'd criticised my wife, I now criticised the court. I can say in favour of my own lawyers that they never made any of these mistakes.

A hearing in a week indeed! She could hold out no hope for *that*! All I got from her was technical language, which, she hoped, would convey some inkling of the court's complexity. It did.

'Good morning,' she said.

180

Farewell Officer! She'd gone. But I felt she still stood there—between my child and his father.

More than a year (sic) passed till the hearing. A sick year. I hoped my wife might meanwhile 'phone to say the child could see me unofficially. Or should *I* do the 'phoning? My solicitor warned against it. I wrote to my child's headmistress to ask if I could see how he was getting on at school, but she replied that this was not possible as in law I was no longer his parent. So he and I continued in total separation.

A fortnight and nothing. Surely his mother would telephone? I'm only a mile away.

What a foul thing is a mile! He's there, and I can't see him, he says words and I can't hear them, he laughs, cries, and I don't know which.

And yet I was with him at all times, even in sleep. An ache under opiate. It was the train I was travelling in, you wake up, and the wheels still rumble under you.

Over you.

I'm another me from the me of seeing my child. No me at all. The walls of my bedsit, the door, the furniture, are white. The light, controlled from outside, is never switched off. My eyelids have been cut away, I feel my head explode, my skull split. My spine drills into my brain, a whole layer of my skin has been ripped off. My body's disintegrating, my soul is pissing away. This is solitary confinement, when even the self has gone—gone dead with hooding and white noise.

I dream I'm in prison, I *am* in prison, unable to move. It's the cell that moves. Judges and registrars cram in, accompanied by barristers and solicitors, scribes and pharisees, they say, *Of course, our primary concern is the child's welfare.*

Ha! Did they say Welfare?

I can't understand it. In Virgil's tenth eclogue even the tamarisks wept for Gallus.

Then a long buff envelope and a copy of the Welfare

Officer's Report. She had seen the child with his mother, there was a very good relationship between them. Naturally she couldn't see him with *me*; but never mind, she could ask the mother, the mother *had* seen him with me.

This Report was submitted to the Royal Courts of Justice. Family Division.

Every day I telephoned to ask the date of the hearing, it was my only conversation. Then, when not more than three months had past, I decided to go out and be sad, it was one of my better days. I wander nowhere, while the rush-hour thickens into evening, and suddenly I feel a frantic need for talk, which is what I've most shunned.

It was now night; but void of darkness, lest thou shouldst miss the grins of happy and united families, who're happy and united because they've chosen the right brand of bread, the right make of mixer. All industry, all technology, are for united and happy families. Without united and happy families there would be no industry, no technology; without industry and technology there would be no united and happy families.

I imagine a whole Atlantis of possibilities whereby I could've stayed with my wife; I plan whole cities, down to the spoons and pillar-boxes, only to watch them sink into the sea.

Dear God, teach me the Greek art of persuasion.

(Without telephoning) I'll just call at the door. I'm your husband. I'm the father of your child. She won't throw me out. How could she? She's seen trees; felt rain.

First I'll have dinner, I need it. Where? All restaurants depress when you're alone: if shabby, they say misery; if smart, sex. Eventually I found something in between, it said sex and misery, I sat down and waited, without even my belly to keep me company, and wondering what to do with my eyes.

Suddenly my body got up and left.

A man stood on the kerb, hailing taxis that weren't free, and every other vehicle as well, not only private cars, but unsuitable things like dustcarts, and buses that wouldn't stop because it wasn't a stop.

I hurried past; past floodlit Georgian stucco, and flats whose loudest sound was the chiming of clocks; till (always unexpectedly) I reached the detritus of North Kensington.

Finally, among those dogs that are half cats, loose after a bitch, and canine excrement on builders' sand, I reach the street I had wanted to buy. Above it, in an erosion of shadow, rises Chivalry House.

The light is on in the kitchen, I can love her. I'll ring the bell. When she sees me on the doorstep of my own house, begging to be let in, she'll forget the alimony, the acrimony.

Except that it isn't my house any longer.

But it's my cunabula; cuniculus. She'll ask me in, won't she? To see the child. Even if she won't allow me to speak to him, surely I can see him? See him while he sleeps. I just want to see him. Watch him grow, undulate upwards.

The worst she can do is tell me to go away.

Is it?

Won't she call the police? I'll again be arrested, and this time I'll have defied a court order, my child will never be allowed to see me again. Haven't I already taken enough risks with him? I made that woman his mother, didn't I?

CHAPTER XVIII

I just stood. My hands strangling each other. Till the light went out.

Only the fine rain held me from unconsciousness.

I caught a pub before closing, it was full of poor decaying creatures, like candles down which wax had dropped; men who spit as a matter of principle, and women of no beauty, or even youth, which is itself a kind of beauty.

'Tell me your trouble,' said a man in a cloth cap.

'I'll feel better with something inside me.'

'Are you a father?'

I looked at him in astonishment. Then I cried and cried, I don't know where the tears came from.

'You must forgive me,' I said. 'There's water enough outside.'

'Mind the beer.'

I laughed.

'Here,' he said, offering me a handkerchief. It smelt of tobacco. 'How many children?'

'One.'

'One's a hundred.'

With most people I shun all talk about my child.

'You can tell I'm a father?'

'What else does a man cry about?'

'You've done your crying?'

'You cry just so much.'

'And no more?'

He drank his beer in ugly gulps, as if it were medicine. 'You then do something about it. My mate went to court with a calf's head and chopped it in two.'

'Was he a crank?'

'He had a point to make.'

'What happened to him?'

'Nothing. The Judge said he was of unsound mind.'

'I've never known a father who wasn't.'

'Why, he asked, did the Judge have to destroy his children. His children were in court, they started screaming, he'd brought them to court, you see.'

'They wanted to stay with him?'

'You can imagine how pleased the Judge was. Tantrums, he called it; and ordered them back to their mother.'

'She'd been given custody, I suppose.'

'Miracle if she hadn't.'

The children, in that case, were extremely impudent; they thought they knew better than the Judge.'

'What's more, they kicked and bit the policeman who came to fetch them.'

'Oh, so they were vicious! That's what happens when children have been with their father.'

'He hasn't been allowed to see them since, and that was two and half years ago.'

'God Almighty!'

'You're not from North Kensington, are you?'

'What?'

'I mean, you don't look like it. Where do you live?'

'What?'

'I expect you live in South Kensington, don't you?'

'Well, I . . .'

'Same as my mate.'

185

'Oh really?'

'I'm from the North of the Borough, see? We don't let women take our children from us in the North of the Borough.'

'No?'

'Not in the North.'

'But the law's no different.'

'In North Kensington we aren't interested in law. Not lawyers' law. Only in justice.'

'You mean you seized your children from their mother?'

'Didn't have to.'

'They came?'

'No, it was she who left. Went off with another man.'

'And so failed to get custody.'

'Don't be daft! Women always get custody. But I said she must bring them back to me, or I and my brothers would come and dust her up, and her lover-boy too while we were about it.'

'So she brought them back?'

'In North Kensington she knows we don't stand no nonsense.'

I too was North Kensington. A proletaire. My wealth was in my offspring. Or so I'd always told myself.

I was North Kensington—failed.

'You must be pleased to have your children.'

'Was.'

'Were they too much for you?'

'My wife and the law between them: it let her take my house away. I'd built it myself. Everything had gone into that house. For my children, really. Children like living in a house. A house is for keeps.'

'At least my child has that,' I said.

'Where is he?'

'Chivalry House.'

186

'Nice.'

'Have your children settled down in their new home?'

'They didn't have a chance. I applied for Council accommodation; and instead of getting it, I lost my children.'

'They were taken from you?'

'Into care.'

'Why?'

'Because fathers can't care.'

Next day I applied to have Chivalry House listed as a building of architectural interest.

The prison authorities are examining the earlier chapters of this book for fear it may jeopardise the forthcoming Opec conference. So I can't check whether I've already told you how I passed the remainder of those thirteen months. I hope I did, for they're now a blank in my memory. So monotonous were they that they seem little more than one day. Morbid and withdrawn, I watched the hours go round and round like a cement-mixer through areas of built-up misery.

Lord God, why must my child's pain be perpetual, and his wound incurable? What guilt I'd felt when away from him one evening! And now his every evening was that one-evening.

My wife may—it's just possible—tell him to write. Each day I meet the postman, but my only mail comes in those long buff envelopes which I'm terrified to open.

Further visits to lawyers. Whom I treat jocularly to get by. Would you bare your heart to a lawyer? Your teeth.

'Your wife may have conducted herself reprehensibly, I'm not saying she didn't; but (this is the question) will the Judge believe it?'

'Probably not. Unless he's carried away by common sense.'

(Leaning back) 'I form the impression that you love your wife less than your child.'

'Than almost anyone.'

'That means you must be particularly careful what you say about her.'

'But I want my child.'

'Do you mean you want . . .?'

'My only hope is to get custody, care and control.'

'Do you know how often custody, care and control are awarded to the father?'

'Once in a blue moon.'

'Once in a blue moon. Precisely.'

'Well?'

'Well, surely there must be a reason for that?'

The question—there's even a smile to go with it—sounds so sage; so civilised; so sweetly reasonable. It's none of these things.

'There's no chance, you mean?'

'We could, if you wish, try for a split order: care and control to the mother, custody to the father.'

'What use is custody without care and control?'

'Frankly, none.'

How I loathe lawyers! Beetles! No, I take that back, I shan't compare them to those little creatures that make their dwelling under stones. I've unhoused too many of them, never meant to.

Apart from lawyers I saw no one. Lived like a monk, with no mirror, but I didn't get up early, sometimes I didn't get up at all. Poor tenants, I understand you!

When shall I see my child? Night and day I never stop seeing him, my nights are days, I'm blind with seeing him.

When shall I see him?

Bound to a stake, facing the sun, I pray for sleep—whether the great sleep of an elephant, or the fine thin sleep of a bird. But was there ever any man seen to sleep in the cart, between Newgate and Tyburn? Perhaps you haven't been in hell. You think it's somewhere you get used to. But each day is the first, and time has different hands.

It was now the hurt end of winter, and the rain fell upon Rotten Row, forging horseshoe puddles, chains of sky in the mud. But on the grass bank, beneath the ancient trees, flowers were reappearing. Another season, and my child still fatherless. Spring. I remembered the poems about spring, which gladdens all creatures except the love-lorn poet. Like him, I 'saw undelighted all delight', and wept at the terrible passage of lost time. The crocuses were those of last year, which my child had likened to the candles on a cake. It's now the first birthday of his total fatherlessness. (Do you know?) I should never have left home. This was the sin for which there's no pardon, and which the very gentiles condemn. I had thought it was the decent thing to do, but now I knew decency was weakness. Decency is sin. All sin is weakness. Even my being sinned against is sin, for she's an artefact of my own making.

Should I ask her forgiveness? Be conciliatory; flower-bringing. Turn the house into a garden and water it with my tears.

'How weak,' she'd say.

But aren't there times when weakness is decency?

I went inside a church, but I felt so alone, as if God himself had lost faith in me. But was it my fault if He forged this female from my rib? If He's so arbitrary, let me be nimble. And yet I'm no Donne to jest Him out of His anger; or Jesuit, with squinting absolution.

How, Lord, would You like to be my child, with one father in heaven and the other in the South of the Borough? Do visit him, no court has denied You access. Give him, please, one day that's as calm and unhaunted as Your dark tent. You're busy, I know, but things must be easing off, now

189

that the Church Militant has shrunk to a corporal's guard; and incidentally I know why: You'll hardly be taken seriously as long as You call Yourself a father and claim to care. Do give the matter thought; but meantime You have at Your disposal the far from meagre resources that omnipotence can supply. And although to alter the past is, I realise, beyond Your capabilities, You may perhaps feel like gathering my wife to Yourself.

CHAPTER XIX

The fact that my petition for a resumption of access did not go unopposed will hardly induce the fair-minded reader to suspect my wife of malice. I have myself admitted that thirteen months divided the injunction from the hearing. Only misconduct of the gravest kind can have necessitated an investigation that takes as long as that. No, I'm certain she was solely motivated by a concern to protect our child. Moreover an exquisite sensitivity toward my own feelings inhibited her from personally stating her case before the court. People have been sent to heaven for less than that.

Nor would I like you to blame the barrister who acted as her mouthpiece. If I say he himself had a child, you may feel puzzled how he could urge the Judge to ban me from ever seeing mine. But be not too hasty; in law, you see, emotion has no place. Barristers—this is their job—must take clients' instructions. Otherwise they will find themselves briefless. And surely you would never wish barristers to be briefless. They love their children; children have mouths; and mouths must be fed.

If there is a fault to find, then find it with the Judge. The child had twitched as long as he had seen me, even if, as was so from the time when I had found it convenient to abandon my wife, he had only seen me when I happened to visit him; but with the denial of access his twitching had ceased. Was it fair on him to renew the nervous tension? Was it fair on the mother who loved him? She threw herself on the mercy of the court. Only the court could protect her child.

In reply the Judge leant over backwards in his seat—an obvious attempt at being fair to me. I don't mean he leant so far backwards as to put me in the witness box after my wife had left it. If a man forces his way into a woman's house, you don't waste the court's time by asking for explanations.

Even so, his lordship was prepared to take a risk—a risk that the general consensus of right-thinking people might incline (with great respect) to call culpable : he granted me access of no less than two and a half hours per week.

True, I didn't actually *see* the child for two and a half hours per week. My wife, for the child's sake, had no option but to take the law into her own hands and say he couldn't see me because he was ill; he couldn't see me because he was going to a children's party; he couldn't see me because he had to catch up with his homework. I saw my solicitor about it, but he said there was very little one could do, short of going back to court, and that would be pointless, because while access could be forbidden it could hardly be enforced. He was terribly sorry.

'Never mind about being sorry,' I said. 'Tell me quite simply : shall I have to pay her more?'

'I couldn't be certain.'

'Of course you couldn't be certain; but what does your experience suggest?'

'You'll have to pay her more.'

'Danegeld. Is that it?'

He smiled. 'Danegeld.'

My initial feeling, let me confess, was one of irritation; but I soon learnt that this was totally unjustified, for it's apparently well known that countless other women behave in the same way. Nor did they have my wife's justification :

she had feared that the child's twitch would return if he ever saw me again. And after a time it did.

I wonder where I went wrong.

My wife, however, didn't go back to court for a new Injunction—possibly because I was now paying her twice the amount of the alimony. 'Yes, you can see him this week,' she said.

I took him to Westminster Hall, where the Lord Chief Justice had resoundingly decided that Shelley's children, their mother being dead, should be forbidden to live with their father.

'What's the time?'

'Good God!'

We were late back. Half an hour late. Her screams!

I said: 'The child's been happy, don't make him miserable.'

The whole of those two and a half hours, no, three, were destroyed in one volley from her mouth. What power of destruction! As if Chivalry House, after all those aeons, should fall to one day's demolition.

I forgot, by the way, to tell you she had now divorced me. On the grounds of cruelty. My lawyers suggested, to my surprise, that I should cross-petition; but they admitted I wouldn't win—and they, for their part, wouldn't have lost. They were concerned about the effect of an undefended action on my friends, and, indeed, my child. I said the sort of friends who would drop me I could well do without; and as for my child, my wife might be able to take him away from me, but she could never take away his love for me, not unless she destroyed nature itself.

I was given custody of the cat.

I was so happy, so sad, that my child could be as close to me as before that year of separation. After each access, back in my bedsit (no bigger than a birdcage) I wept for my child, who, with the run of the largest house and garden in North Kensington, was as trapped as I was—trapped in those two and a half hours that his lordship, in the Royal Courts of Justice, Family Division, had allowed us for seeing each other—just long enough to freshen the joy, and short enough to torture.

'Teach me to bowl,' he said. But two and a half hours aren't long enough. In any case, it isn't two and a half hours, there's the getting anywhere and the getting back. And he couldn't concentrate because he kept worrying about the time. 'What's the time? Will we be back in time?'

My child! No twitch, at least. And yet his eyes looked strange, as if he were unused to this particular planet.

I bought an old car, £500 or very nearly. Garaging was another ten pounds a week. Without breakfast. But in future we wouldn't spend our whole two and a half hours waiting for buses. 'Where do you want to go?'

'Along the M1,' he said, climbing all over the dashboard.

'Where to, though?'

'Just along it.'

'And then?'

'Then back.'

He liked being in the car with me. We were co-conspirators.

While we took the road out of London, noisy and noxious, he asked me the sex of angels. And why the Marquis of Granby had so many pubs. He didn't like other cars to overtake us, and when I said they were exceeding the limit, he said if *they* were *we* could.

'How're you getting on at school?'

'All right. Why don't you have automatic gear-change?'

'Made any friends?'

'They say you and Mummy aren't real parents.'

194

'Why not?'

'Because you don't live together.'

'That's not your fault.'

He was silent. Why had I mentioned 'fault'? There're certain ideas one shouldn't put into a child's head. Except that they're there already.

He said : 'Nine twelves.'

'What?'

'You heard.'

'Hundred and eight.'

'Slow.'

'Listen, if the other boys laugh at you, tell them they're unchristian.'

Next week I asked him if they were still laughing.

'Yes.'

'Did you tell them they were unchristian?'

'Yes.'

'And what did they say?'

'They laughed more than ever.'

'Did they?'

'Yes. So what shall I do?'

'Hack their shins.'

Decency is weakness.

Poor child! But at least he wasn't twitching.

'What's school dinner like?'

He replied : 'In jail you only get bread and water.'

'Oh?' I said. Unless my wife were the Governor, and then you'd be offered a choice of one or the other. 'I don't suppose it's as bad as that.'

'About the same as school.'

We went to the Zoo, explored the animals that have nothing to explore : the pacing up and down of the cheetah; the stylised masturbation of baboons; the gorilla that prods his ears with straw; the elephant that nods his head for hours

195

on end. Creatures biting themselves, pulling out their hair.

'Don't tread on the crocodile,' I said; 'you may find it isn't a crocodile at all, but a log, and you know how easy it is to fall off a log.'

That amused him. 'Say something else that's funny.'

'Do you know why kings and queens make England so wet?'

'They keep reigning. Cinch.'

Those were my better jokes. I shall draw a veil over the others.

He was now starting to twitch again. I hugged him in my arms, hoping to cure him, but he stiffened, drew away as soon as I released him. I 'phoned his mother, asked her what she thought was troubling him. Two and a half hours was so short, I could give him the odd treat, but this wasn't being a father to him. It was being Father Christmas.

Her answer was: 'You must abide by the Judge's decision.'

Would it be better if I could save up a dozen of these two-and-a-half-hour accesses and have them in one go? But he might not want to be with me for so long: being with me meant *not* being with his mother.

So we continued with the usual access; the access that was no access. Is a molecule of sugar, sugar?

He played with me in the park, he played football, played catch, and now always played the tough guy, though so tender, so in need of tenderness.

He sketched the view, his hand jogged with the twitches.

'My child!' I said. I said it aloud, I shouldn't have said it aloud.

'Drat and double drat!'

'What's wrong?'

'Give me a rubber.'

'Why do you need a rubber?'

196

'I've made a mistake.'
'No, you haven't.'
'Yes, I have.'
'Show me.'
'There, blind man!'
'That's not a mistake.'
'What is it, then?'
'A *pentimento*.'
'Yikes!'
'People pay the earth for a *pentimento*.'
'What's the time?' he said.
'Time for tea.'
'Let's have potatoes in their jackets.'
He liked potatoes in their jackets—the phrase and the thing.
We took a bus.
He said: 'Where's your car?'
'I sold it.'
'Why?'
'Hard up.'
'Hard cheese!'
'You'll have to help me bake the potatoes, I've only got two pairs of hands.'
'You mean *one* pair!'
'One pair.'
'One apple.'
'Besides a potato in its jacket you want an apple as well?'
'I want six.'
'Six? Goodness me! Apples don't grow on trees, you know.'
'Yes, they do!'
I unlocked the door of my bedsit. 'You must give me a hand.'

197

'Left or right.'

I chased him round the room, seized him. 'I've got you, you'll never escape.'

'Yes, I shall!'

'No, you won't.'

'Told you!'

'Let's see your drawing.'

'What was that word?'

'*Pentimento*.'

'Can you see the boat we sailed in?'

'And there's the *pentimento*, moored alongside it.'

'What's the time?'

'Nearly time to go.'

'It's raining again, why does it always rain.'

'Rain's lovely, it comes straight from heaven.'

'You could've fooled me.'

We took the bus back to the house.

'Daddy,' he said, 'where do you live? I mean the address, I've forgotten it.'

And a woman who was sitting beside us overheard him, smiled to herself. There's something terribly sweet about a child who asks where his father lives. Particularly a child so tiny, whose feet don't even reach the floor of the bus, they shake with the shaking.

I said goodbye at the gate. 'A pity it's so short always.'

Might he interpret that as criticism of his mother. I must never say anything that he could interpret as criticism of his mother.

I so wanted to hug him. '(Do you realise?) only my body goes. I'm with you in spirit. This house has been my home from birth. Still is. Always will be. And it's yours too. I've made sure no one can ever take it away from us.'

He bent down and pulled at the wet grass till his fingers were green. 'It's a horrid house,' he said. And ran down the path. I thought he might turn and wave as he reached the door. He didn't, though.

I remained at the gate, said hello to my plants, who seemed undismayed, but I doubted the sincerity of their indifference. Fears were winding up inside me, and within a week the Managing Director of Bethell explained how I would never have been asked to join the board if I hadn't owned property in the very area they planned to develop. But now I had not only sold out, but moved to the other end of the Borough. Might it not, in a very real sense, be more meaningful if I were to tender my resignation?

CHAPTER XX

When I next fetched my child, bulldozers were scooping around the house. My plants were buried alive; or left crushed and crippled. My garden had gone. And what could I do but curse? Bethell! Lord God, not Bethlehem, shall I spell it for You? *Bet*; as in risk. And *hell*. As in marriage.

I have a gentlemen's agreement with them, I shake hands with them over the port, they're to preserve my house for ever. And they destroy my garden. Isn't the garden a part of the house?

Yet my child didn't care. I'd have been sorry if he'd cared. I was sorrier as he didn't. But I behaved cheerfully to him for those two and a half hours, though repeatedly making mistakes like pushing doors marked *Pull*.

And he laughed. 'Can't read.'

The garden had gone, my mind was hopelessly trying to re-create it, I watched my hopelessness, I was an insect that had fallen on its back, I was those interminably clumsy efforts to right itself.

I 'phoned my solicitor. 'If the house is listed, they can't touch the garden, can they?'

'No,' he said. 'Don't worry. It's within the curtilage.'

'Curtilage be damned! They're bulldozing it!'

What had been my garden was soon sprouting a ten-storey block. And my child and his mother moved into the top flat.

Below it, as yet unfinished, were nine other flats. They were the flats that built her flat.

What consolation had I? Only that the house itself couldn't be touched. Or so I thought. But immediately, though it was a listed building, Bethell applied for permission to demolish. It was refused. So the airspace on that prime site continued to be wasted—unless Bethell took the law into their own hands; it would be morally wrong not to.

There's no longer a Chivalry House. It takes courage to do what Bethell did—they demolished a listed building. The authorities, as was foreseen, expressed their disapproval. Refused planning permission.

And the wound remained an open one.

It remained open long enough for grass to grow.

My child never took my hand again. He didn't even want rough play, because it would mean touching me. He now saw me as little as once a month. If I complained to his mother she said she couldn't force him. It wouldn't be right to. He was old enough to make up his own mind.

Yet still quite often he could be happy with me, whether tiger or lamb, though there was so little we could do in two and a half hours. I never took him out of London, we would never walk over downs, swim in the sea, smell sheep. And now, at home, he didn't even have trees to climb.

He didn't even have home. Yet for eighteen months its site remained as a reminder. And then the authorities let Bethell have their way. They had to in the end. It would've been morally wrong not to.

I telephoned my wife. 'Is the child all right?'

Silence. The sort of silence that was invented by the telephone.

'For Christ's sake!' I said.

'If he's all right it isn't thanks to you.'

'I trust he can't hear what you're saying.'

She screamed. *Why* had the house suddenly been listed, she wanted to know. What a father I was!

The housing boom—I'd almost ceased following such things—crashed as quickly as it had arisen. Building costs had doubled, and the banks were refusing to lend any more money. So the blocks of flats that had been going up on the site of Chivalry House—it'd have been *finished* but for my tomfoolery—remained a *shell*. And who's going to buy a shell? How would I like to be paying interest at $16\frac{1}{2}\%$ and nothing coming *in*? I hadn't *saved* the house by getting it listed. But eighteen months were lost before Bethell could build. And that made the difference between boom and slump—between a fortune and bankruptcy.

'Sorry I can't pay,' I said.

She screamed : 'I'll make you *pay* all right.'

She had the child.

My days and nights were the same colour, the colour of fear. Would she be beating him till Saturday came? And when Saturday came, would I see him?

He wasn't at the door, he was usually at the door, I knocked, he came to the window. I waved.

He didn't wave back, but remained motionless, expressionless, except for the twitch, and the grimace that went with it.

As much as a minute before he moved.

And now that he was finally at the door, was I to tell him off? I saw him so little, was I to spend that little on telling him off? Was I to tell him off when the fault wasn't his? Was I to let it pass, let him think it was right to behave as his mother taught him?

'You should wave back when I wave to you.'

He didn't answer. What right had I to reprimand him when I was wicked?

202

I watched his fingers tremble, as if they were suffering from some elaborate denial.

'Well, never mind. You're a good boy, really. What would you like to do?'

He shrugged. Looked old.

'Come on,' I said; 'pull yourself together.'

'I'm not in pieces.'

His eyes are glass, he's further away than away. 'Careful you don't walk into a lamp-post,' I said.

'You can't walk *into* a lamp-post.'

As I confronted his hostile eyes I remembered their devotion.

Yet he should've been so happy, we were down on the sand by Tower Bridge, and quite by chance the bascules opened to receive HMS Norfolk, Britain's biggest, best, and only battleship.

'We're in luck!' I said. 'Isn't it exciting?'

'Thrill,' he said. My child! After all your centuries of waiting, my centuries of hoping, you now find yourself in hate.

Upstream the Oxford crew were training in the distance.

'How perfect!' I said. 'As if there were only one oar on either side.'

'I hope Cambridge win,' he said.

I had no word or look from him except such as tear flesh.

Never again was he easy to please. If he told his mother I'd introduced him to new people, she said: 'Always strangers.' If people he'd met before: 'Not *them* again!' If grown-ups: 'Old people, what company for a child!' If other children: 'That's because he has no friends.'

How, you ask, do I know this. Do you think I can't detect her tone in him? That woman, that woman! She could draw poison out of manna.

We passed two dogs, they were fighting over a bone. He stopped; hoped they would get hurt.

At school he got into trouble for bashing another boy. My child, I know how you feel! If I decided to be specially kind to my cat in the hope that one creature's happiness could infect another's, I also decided to be cruel to it, so that there might be some cruelty my child didn't suffer.

He said : 'You've never been a good father.'

'Oh?' I said. 'Why do you think that?'

'Everybody says so.'

'Then how do I have any friends?'

'They don't know what you're like.'

I felt such a smother of affection. Your father's always been bad, his mother had told him. And he'd answered : Then how does he have any friends? My child, I can see it all!

Back in my bedsit I made him tea, said things I hoped would amuse him. But he was mistrustful of everything; withdrew. It was a kind of death. His eyes were caged. And I remembered his years of faith; I'd never known such faith; no, not in Israel. Every beat of his heart had once said thank you for my love. But now, if I rolled it all up into one ball and threw it at him in a game of catch, he'd only swerve to avoid it.

'Would you like to play ball after tea?' I said.

'Will you please stop talking, and get the cake, that's if there *is* any cake, meantime I'd like another crumpet, may I have one, I've helped myself already, thank you.'

What am I to do? Punish him because of her? I've had enough of punishing him because of her. We want a little justice.

I took him back home; to a home where his whole life was set apart for hate.

'See you next week,' I said.

He shrugged. 'If you want to.' Hadn't he once begged me to come every day? (Surprisingly) my wife was no longer preventing him from seeing me. I think she knew what pain it caused me.

CHAPTER XXI

I must find moments of forgetting. In drink. Fellatio with strangers. Applying for jobs I'd never get.

I look in the mirror, see Old Sarum in a storm.

What can I do to stay sane? I learn that climbing up the wall, and banging your head against it, are apt metaphors. No metaphors at all.

I long for night, night is holier than day, if night weren't day. Can I dull myself to the dreadful? God, if You're God, strike that woman, if she's a woman. Yes, she's a woman. I shan't insult the great Prince of Darkness by calling her Satan. I felt her very existence and perdurance contaminated history, and even jeopardised the stars. First she took my child from me. Then she took away his love for me. Would *you* have done that? Would you put out the eyes of a lynx?

I spent whole days hating; nights, too. I'd pull out her hairs, one by one, even her eyelashes.

I remembered how, almost before he could walk, he would run to me, throw his arms around my neck. I thought such things were dead for centuries. And I murmured lines of Virgil to ease the pains of joy. Such closeness! With his body at my chest, he might've been inside me, content to lodge in me unborn. We were one body; but now I myself was no longer one body. My heart beats in my head, in my arms and legs too, they too have hearts, hearts that're heads.

A telephone rings in the next bedsit, and clocks simultaneously are striking the hour. 'Child!' I say. This once promised so much; but now it's 'Christ', and 'Hell', and all oaths spoken in vain.

Only next week, while we were walking along, he took my hand. Naturally, he wasn't thinking what he was about. I looked at him with love. Then he remembered he was doing something he shouldn't, and his hand withdrew.

At once all the traffic of London seemed to go down the wrong way; and in a voice I'd never heard from him, though I'd heard it from his mother, he said: 'You treat me like a dog.'

(I can't understand it) I was terribly calm. 'Treat me like a dog? What makes you think that?'

'You say to me "Good boy." "Good boy" is what people say to dogs.'

I then said—I was certain already, so I don't know why I said it—I said: 'What a funny thing to say! I'm sure your mother would laugh if you told her that.'

'It was she who said it.'

Suddenly my body became rigid, as if divided from its own breathing. Though she'd committed worse crimes, this, I knew instantly, was the unforgivable one. I would suffer it no longer. It was time she moved down the bus.

I took him back before the two and a half hours were up. 'I love you always,' I said.

He didn't answer. It seemed the whole world's sap had sunk.

I found a call box, rang my wife. 'Listen,' I said.

But she hung up.

What could I do? I used the only means of communication that remained open to me: I murdered her.

Not then. I waited till hate became rage. Rage is sweeter than hate.

207

Bobbies patrolled, I turned into an alley. A tenant in a dark room was reading by the light of a street lamp.

The alley echoed with footsteps, but not a footstep was there. *All* footsteps were there—approaching, receding; as if pacing out eternity.

As soon as midnight struck, I was at the unfinished block of flats that stood where my plants had once grown—windows upon windows, like the open eyes of the dead.

I took the lift to the top floor. Rang the bell. Heard her footsteps approach the door. She opened it. Only an inch, then it crunched against the chain. 'All right,' I said, 'it's me.' My toe was in the door, my shoulder against it, the chain gave. 'You won't scream, will you? Think of the child.'

She was so calm. Her only hope was to stay calm. 'What do you want?'

I looked at her beauty. I'd forgotten how beautiful she was. But a beauty of the wrong kind: a Brasilia; there was nothing ancient about her—built where no roads meet, except Admiration and Loathing.

'Tell me what you want,' she said.

'I've come to murder you.'

Her hand ran through her hair. 'Obviously there's something we ought to discuss.'

I won't kill her. The flat's well looked after. She makes sure the child's fed, has clean clothes. If she had only handed him one crust of bread, I would spare her for that charity.

Yet within the District of Weimar lay Buchenwald.

'I'll pour you a whisky,' she said.

'You don't seem concerned.'

'Oh, but I *am* concerned. Supposing the police saw you. I ask them to keep an eye on the place. It's a crime for you to be here.'

'There's only one crime,' I told her. 'Cruelty. And the worst crime is cruelty to children.'

'But what about breaking people's doors down? Is that a decent thing to do?'

'Decency is weakness.'

'Women're liable to scream, you know.'

'I *do* know.'

'And the child would hear.'

'Yes, I seem to remember.'

'So leave.'

'If people are cruel to children they must pay.'

I smelt the fear on her. 'No, don't.'

'Why not?'

'Think of the child.'

'Take off your clothes,' I said.

And she did, almost at once, as if that was what she'd been waiting for.

Her skin was the colour of distant snow.

'Make love to me,' she said. 'If I've been nasty to you, it's only because I love you.'

'You're a good girl,' I said.

Motionless and mute, she eyed my meaning, I think she'd already guessed, she had a marvellous intelligence. 'Good girl?'

'To a dog you say "Good boy".'

She smiled. It was a pretty smile, like dawn out-breaking.

And I made love with her.

She said : 'You're the whole world to me.' And perhaps I was. But she spent me all at once.

Then she disappeared into the bathroom, as if to wash away the whole sad past. 'You'd better go. Come back another time.'

(Following her) 'I haven't finished.'

She said : 'Do you love me?'

'No,' I said.

'Please, it's time you left, do as I say.'

I shook my head. 'It's I, madam, who'll direct this little scene.' And I got her rave reviews.

I turned on the taps, hot and cold, made sure the water was a pleasant temperature. 'Get in the bath,' I said.

Her flesh caught the meaning from my tone, every pore was alert. 'Are you a madman?' she said, eyeing the exact danger.

Should I give her time to repent? Our critical day is not the very day of our death, but the whole course of our life.

Suddenly my conditioned reflexes, with no drug but the will, lost their inhibitions. I seized her, she fought, I fought too, fought my nausea.

Think clearly, the child's asleep, he must sleep, so at his mother's first in-draw of breath I'll (don't worry) abort her scream.

But she didn't scream; she couldn't; her mouth in a moment was quite dry, and her tongue was fastened to the roof of it. She was stiff; she seemed already dead; and her hands were ice, she had died the death of fear.

But her heart still beat, pounding against the bars of its cage.

Till I drowned her. She was dead. Her acres were shrunk to those few perishable feet.

She knew she was dead. And yet—still the ambition to rise—an ambition so big in that small body. Her hands grasped air and bath, and knew not the difference. By some last exercise of the will she again tried to get up, it was no use, but she tried. Here was human will, when it's reduced to the common denominator of all will, the will we share with every other species, the honour of the beast.

Then the air turned tepid, and she lapsed into unknowing.

Time stood still, I don't know how long, it was jellified. Then suddenly it jumped, like a broken typewriter.

210

A low, private cry, she made a good corpse. A sinking back into the bath—her limbs seeming to dispose themselves with a peculiar care. And when she was already dead, her eyes opened, they were in search of my face, but they couldn't get it, my face was a blur in the shape of a face. Then they focused, gave my own eyes a final look, as if defeat were a kind of victory.

She was dead. And I too was diminished. If you've made love with someone and he dies, he'll take part of you with him to the grave.

Lord God, Eternal Father, Father of the fatherless, I'd prayed for this hour; tierce and nones had past.

It took twenty-seven minutes. I timed myself. A life of dying had been too short.

Do you imagine she and my hate died together? I wanted to strip her skin, that soft flesh, I wanted to see the bare bone, hear the hard clankety-clank before the wheels went over me.

About killing, as in engendering, there's something magical that transcends the human.

You think I killed her for the kick? There she lies. Was that the mother of my child, that strange toy in the bath? From now on I'll neither help nor harm her, I'll ignore her, not piss on her body, no, not even if it was on fire.

I go to the window, let in fresh air, look down on the lines of lamps, silver in the side streets, amber in the arteries, dissolving into the galactic whisps of Hampstead and High-gate, as if faint stars had fallen into the lower part of the sky. Such silence! Except for the tick of the church clock, pre-ternaturally I could hear the tick of the church clock, it knocked every second on the head as it was born. Then the clock struck. And *struck* is the right word, the strokes were piercing, with no roundness to them. Followed by an intense hush. And in it the sounds of evening dropped, it was like the

211

time before birth, the only colour was that of a pale and heavy dread.

Shall I take my child?

Torch-flash behind me. I turned. A Bobby.

Between me and the child.

He said : 'What're you doing here?'

'There's a corpse inside.'

'Man or woman?'

'She's not a woman if she's dead,' I answered. She's a job for the pathologist, a fee for the undertaker.

'Did you kill her?'

'Yes,' I said. To lie seemed so mundane.

'Who is she?'

'My wife.'

He frowned. 'Your *wife*?' He was very young. Who else does one kill?

'My *late* wife, I should presumably say—though that sounds a little ungracious, for her one positive trait was punctuality.'

'You can tell me about her without speaking ill.'

'That, I'm afraid, would leave me with remarkably little to say.'

CHAPTER XXII

No, I shan't bore you with details of the trial. There's no need to. I'm famous.

The trouble with fame is that it prevents you from being known.

Guilty, or not guilty.

Not guilty: I did it.

But I *was* guilty. In killing her I was frustrating the Judge's favouritism; I was breaking the consular fasces.

Of course, I had a defending counsel, but he was committed to principles that placed him among the prosecutors. In his mouth my own words took sides against me. It wasn't merely murder that I was tried for: I was tried for my whole life. For gardening. For failing to exploit tenants. For visiting my child when my wife had told me he was ill.

I was tried for having married a saint. She was a saint. The witnesses proved it, telling all they knew about her, and rather more.

The Judge never asked me to explain myself. He didn't even make the mistake of trying to reconstruct things under the lamp. He didn't try at all.

Looked angry.

Every man to his trade.

As far as I can make out, my greatest crime was a failure to show remorse. This I refused to do. To claim you're wicked when you aren't is the worst form of hypocrisy. Mourn the death of my wife? I can only mourn the life of my child.

My child! He sprang to my lips in moments of strange prayer.

The Judge summed up with much morality, and I thought he might've let me off with a caution. But he sentenced me to death. Or life. What's the difference? And he called me all sorts of names, mostly the names of rather gentle and harmless animals that I've always loved, like the pig.

My name you'll find in Roget under brute.

Only now did the Judge ask me if I had anything to say. No, my lord, I'll waste no sentence on you. My hate I reserve for those who see two sides to every question, even when there's only one side; for those who pity me, denying my right of choice, seeing no monster in me because I can't be human; who blame the peer group, the System, the id, the very stars. I have no sympathy with sympathy of that sort. It ranks me below the common mugger.

Ye soul-destroying intellectuals! Give me back Tyburn, burn my bowels before my face, this were compassion, compliment.

I'm in prison for life. I didn't appeal. Life imprisonment, I realise, is the price for murder.

Unless you're a woman, and then it's psychiatric treatment. For some kinds of murder there's nothing at all.

They take me to prison. I'm first put in a waiting-room. All prison is a waiting-room. Then the allotted cell. Myself a cell. Walled up in a rotting body. A number in an interminable gallery. With God alone. Like God along. Without comfort of creatures, or creature comforts. Where night and masturbation are my only tendernesses. What purpose can my life have? Except to point the moral of some hideous tale: I did the right thing, and did it too late.

Again the sun goes down behind the perimeter wall, but you don't visit me, my child. The post each morning; but from you, for me, none. Yet I write to you daily from my dwindling tunnel of self. Won't you give me an outside?

You too are inside. Inside a Home. Not a *real* home, because they don't denounce me.

They never mention me.

That too is a form of denunciation.

I know why you don't come: they won't let you. They hope thereby to kill me. They won't. One day that small door will let me out.

Will you see me? If only to look hate at me. But you *have loved*. Therefore you love. I'll see through you. Yet if the hate were to fall away and only the love remain, I'd still mourn. The human race is itself transitional; and perhaps some other beings will say, when only a few bones of us remain, What does it all matter? It matters, my child, because it *has been*. I remember (though not where) a fragment of Alexandrian papyrus, telling how a child threw stones at passing people. I feel sorry for the child, sorry for the people. You'll tell me what's past is past. Quite! Therein lies the sadness; no sadness is so sad as sadness that's unavailing.

I envy the men who tread the yard with me, their children wait for them, I envy their children. But my own child imbibed hate from his mother's breasts, the left and the right, it's part of his tissue.

My child, don't hate me. I'll pick up the bits of you, bit by bit, pained, painstaking, like the plates your mother threw at me. I want you to be happy, and hate is so sad. Daily I weep for your lost happiness and lasting pain. This—not prison—is my sentence.

And it's a sentence I accept. I'd take double if it could help you. I'd even take the final torture of all, the doubt whether I should go on loving you. That at least I've been spared.

Should I love you less because you've been taught to hate me? My love is only the more, and topped with pity. My child, I'll treat you like a dog; I'll treat a dog as if he were my only child; and both as if the world depended on them.

Ungentle woman! Specious monster, my accomplished snare! She crucified me. Then sent in a bill for the nails.

And now flowers visit her tomb.

If only she'd nurtured my child with half the love she lavished on her own bitterness.

Repent, says the chaplain.

Repent my one good deed?

Forgive her, then.

To forgive *her* would rob forgiveness of all meaning.

The calendar says March, the flowers lighten the grass of Kensington Gardens, they're the candles on a birthday cake. Another year. But the outside seems farther away as my legs get older; my release draws no nearer as the sun slows down. I no longer measure time in days, or space in miles, but both in fatigue. My face is cracked ivory. Flies, running over it, have been known to break their ankles. But when I'm put out on the street, free to beg my bread from door to door, old, larval and consumed, with no carnal passion but the fear of draughts, (I wonder) will my child still be alive, or will he have died of all those negatives? And shall I, as if he were an expendable item, look for another woman, another artefact, who'll work with my nature? She'll say: 'Take off your clothes.' And she'll see the veins stand like foothills on my feet, no body but a lifeless armature of bone. Yet perhaps like the entombed grain of the Egyptians, I'll sprout after centuries. She'll call my love of gardening no defect; or my love of child either—not that he'll be a child any longer.

But he'll always be *my* child.

Some fathers may forget. I'm not in their list. When the sun has burnt itself out, and our planet has joined the majority, I trust to have full sight of him in heaven without restraint. And when he asks me, not angrily, why his mother had to die, I'll say it was so that the shadows could fall north at noon, and the beetles move along the dirt beneath the disposable cans and cartons.

Wicked woman! Though I and not you am in prison, do you hope to escape the judgement of God?

Are you not afraid?

But I, unhumbled, unrepentant, unreformed, already at the worst, fear nothing. And hope in my old age to see my child, and feel his arms about me.

And we shall reign past thy preventing.